BEYOND THE
LATCH AND LEVER

First Glimma Publishing edition 2020

Published by Glimma Publishing, Trondheim, Norway
glimmapublishing.com

Interior design by Erik Amundsen
Cover design by Elle Blackwood / elleblackwood.com

Printed in the United States of America

ISBN: 978-82-691325-1-9

BEYOND THE
LATCH AND LEVER

Edited by

**Susanna Skarland
and Elle Blackwood**

glimma publishing
Trondheim Norway

OTHER BOOKS BY GLIMMA PUBLISHING

A Map of My Existence by Elle Blackwood

SHORT SYNOPSES

Esterbell (© 2020) Elle Blackwood: An old woman returns to the crumbling French château where she spent her childhood to say goodbye to the keeper of her past.

The Two Lives of Agapito Cortez (© 2020) Carlos Joaquin Gonzalez: A wounded, Mexican-born Union soldier awakens to find the world isn't the same as he remembers.

The Third Quirk (© 2020) Karin Larsen: An alien retrieves their dead brother's spaceship and comes to terms with their grief.

Home to Skjolden (© 2020) Erik Amundsen: When a man returns to Northern Norway to sell his family's farm, a curious encounter unearths the past and makes him question his legacy.

Flight of the Bumblebee (© 2020) Susanna Skarland: A young couple in the near future struggle to survive in a world where the natural pollinators have died off and corporate robotics serve as their replacement.

Liminality (© 2020) R. L. Castle: An elderly doormaker seeks comfort in the doors of his past.

Between Hell and Fire (© 2020) Bobbie Peyton: A young Filipina farmworker must navigate the haunting nature of racism on an asparagus farm in 1960s California.

The Pantry Ghost (© 2020) H. K. Porter: Trapped inside an unfamiliar pantry, a young woman struggles to piece together the string of events that led to her isolation.

Rabbit's Key (© 2020) Steve Garriott: When a physics major agrees to an adventure with an eccentric young man, they stumble upon a scientific discovery that alters their reality and their futures.

The Last Door in the Hilbert Hotel (© 2020) Evvan Land: A man must complete a test to find the exit from his own personal hell.

The Wending Way (© 2020) J. S. Artz: A celestial being sent to Earth must decide whether to stay and help, or leave humankind to their own destruction.

To Rob, my love, who suffered through many late-night dinners and early morning meetings. More chocolate for you. To all my family, friends, and mentors who have supported me along this writing and editing journey— thank you. As always, take a chance, open the door. –**Susanna**

Para mi Chico—my clever, witty son who knows the Latin root of every-thing. And for Isbjørnen min—my brilliant, unflappable husband who finds the plot when I lose it. Thanks to you guys, I have everything I need. Apart from a Dutch door. I would really like a Dutch door. **—Elle**

CONTENTS

INTRODUCTION

Magic lives inside of doors.

What?

Okay, doorways. Thresholds. When two things come together and energies collide, it creates an *in-between*. A liminal space. This is where a door hangs—where magic lives. Anything can happen. Discoveries are made, promises exchanged. Possibilities are endless. A doorway can be a bridge, a crossroads, or a precipice. A passageway leading somewhere unknown. Doorways can be portals between two realities, two eras, two worlds. They transport us to the past or usher us into the future.

Throughout history and across cultures, doors have been celebrated and feared, and heavily guarded. People protect doorways with rituals and spells. With amulets, dragons, and gargoyles. There are rusty doors, carved doors, and cellar doors. Shed doors, trap doors, and hatch doors. Doors made of mahogany panels, glass panes, or solid stone. Doors that appear and disappear.

Doors are entrances and exits, beginnings and endings. They

offer great privacy and protection or leave us isolated and confined. There are doors we slam shut, and doors we open wide. Doors we run to, and doors we creep away from. There are doors that shut out demons—and doors that don't.

Some doors are obliging. They shed light through their gaps or offer keyholes and cracks we can peek throuh, hoping to glimpse people, places, secrets—whatever lies on the other side. Other doors remain dark and foreboding. Mysterious. They are obstacles to negotiate. Opportunities just out of reach. Barriers and boundaries meant to overcome. Doors can make us desperate. Do we turn back, defeated? Or push onward and knock, ring the bell, or pound our fists. Something—anything—to hear the latch click and see the lever turn. But some doors remain locked forever unless you hold the key.

In this book you will find eleven doors. Eleven stories waiting to be opened. Each one a passageway into the unknown.

Elle and Susanna

ESTERBELL

Elle Blackwood

Let's begin with an old woman in a black sedan. She sits alone in the backseat, staring at the gatehouse through the foggy glass. Crumbling stones, broken windows, twisted iron fences—the scars cut deep.

The old woman recognizes the waxy green hedges, now ragged and overgrown, but the landscape beyond is unfamiliar. The woods are darker. Deeper. These aren't the images flooding her dreams. Why did she wait so long to return? She's made excuses over the years, but none of them made sense. The truth? Had the old woman come back, she wouldn't have left again.

The driver sticks his head out the window and cranes his neck. Does he have enough clearance? It's a close call. Not worth a scraped fender. He shifts into reverse, and a cool breeze stirs the hedges along the road. Buttery petals float through the open window and the car is filled with fragrant citrina—a scent that carries memories of his grand-mère.

Fingers drum against the gearshift. The driver doesn't want to disappoint the kind woman in the backseat. He shifts back into gear, holds his breath, and inches the car through the rusted gates. Relaxing his shoulders again, he starts up the long driveway, weaving around deep pools of muddy water carved by rain. He mumbles under his breath, but the old woman isn't listening. It's the first day of fall, and she's forgotten her yellow headscarf.

Yellow? The old woman fixes her eyes on the soft glow of the dashboard. This reminds her of something, but what? Her vision blurs as she sifts through the dusty images of her childhood. And there it is—the first day she arrived. Her bed was next to a pretty girl with flaxen hair and rosy cheeks. Marielle? Mariette? The girl was older than her—by six months? A year? She can't remember, but the girl was at least seven on account of the yellow ribbon in her hair. The old woman had worn a pale blue ribbon because she was only six, but she envied the soft lemon chiffon. When her seventh birthday came around and they gave her a yellow ribbon, the rosy-cheeked girl was gone.

This is where her story began. Once upon a time, the old woman had one name: Esterbell.

The sedan climbs the twisted curves up the hill. Just before they reach the top, the road disappears under a carpet of twigs and leaves. On either side of the road, the trees have grown thick as walls, and there's a ceiling of bowed branches where a sky should be. Does he have room to turn around? It would be difficult at best. The driver glances through the rear-view mirror, unsure if he should proceed. Ester gives a fateful nod, and the car slips into the mouth of the tunnel. Darkness soaks up every drop of light.

They pull into a circular driveway riddled with weeds, and Ester sucks in her breath. Before the driver reaches her door, she's out of the car, staring at a steep-pitched roof crowded with jagged spires, pinnacles, and massive chimneys reaching high in the air to clear the iron cresting. Her gaze drops to the crumbling round towers and charred stone walls of Château Mara, a Gothic castle she once called home. A shell of a fairy-tale.

"Sacrebleu! You've fallen ill." She stares into Mara's vacant, eye-like windows, and a loose shutter creaks against the breeze. "They told me, but I did not want to believe." Her voice is barely a whisper, but the château is listening. She's sure of it.

Tick. Tick. Tick.

A tightness fills Ester's chest, and she rests her hand against the timepiece just below the surface. The ticks are sharp and erratic. She must steady the pendulum.

"Madame?"

The driver hands Ester the walking stick she left in the back-seat, and she glances at the silver nametag pinned to his suit coat. *Jules Clochette.*

"Merci, Monsieur Clochette." She gives him a faint smile and wedges the point of her blackthorn stick between wet tufts of grass.

Ester fills her lungs and tastes the loamy soil and earthy moss. The rotting wood and wet stone. The scent of the château saturates the surrounding woodlands and seeps into the valley below. It crosses the rolling green fields and blankets the village who turned his back on her ages ago. On both of them.

Nature has reclaimed much of the château. Aside from the grand arched entry and the windows on either side, small trees and shrubs obscure the entire first floor. The gargoyle who guards the massive front door is still visible. Perched atop the portico's stone archway, his grotesque face and lurching pose were meant to strike fear into the hearts of unwanted guests. As a young girl, Esterbell trembled each time she crossed under the arch. Later, when she learned the gargoyles protected the children from demons roaming outside, she invited one to live in her mind. Her very own gargoyle to fight off the demons roaming her past.

Jules stands tall near the front of the sedan. His cap is pulled firmly over his curls, and he's dressed in a tailored black suit, a crisp white shirt, and a charcoal tie that matches the lingering clouds. His face is pleasant. Honest. His expression is somber, but when he smiles, his eyes light up. When did he last smile like that? He can't recall. It's been quite a while.

He looks about thirty-five, but Jules turns forty next month. He's single, at least he will be soon, and he doesn't have kids. He's completely ruined his chances for that. There *is* a part of him that wants a family, but it's only a sliver. What if he's no better than his parents? He won't risk it, so he keeps the sliver wedged deep, where it stays hidden. Sometimes even from himself.

Ester's white hair flutters in the wind as she gazes up at a center tower stretching two hundred feet in the air like a long dragon neck. At the top, sits a golden clock, the face of Mara, and behind the tower is her massive body, flanked by the castle's two enormous wings. For a moment, Ester wonders if the château might fly away, and she wishes it would. Like an injured beast who lay dying, no one dares get close to Mara's prickly exterior. The château is running out of time. Other French castles share the same fate, but this is the castle Ester cares about.

Tick. Tick. Tick.

"Do you see them?" she whispers. Blood whooshes through her ears.

Ester's heart-shaped face and soft voice remind Jules of his grand-mère. How he misses her coq au vin and her chocolate soufflé.

Her logical advice, and the warmth in her eyes when Jules asked about his parents. For a long time, his grand-mère was his only family. His root to the past. Since her death, he's been floating. His feet rarely touch the ground for long.

"See what, Madame?" There are so many details, Ester could be referring to anything.

"The saplings." She cranes her neck and points to the roof, her hand stiff with arthritis. "Do you see them up there? Growing in the turrets?" There's a pleading in her voice. She wants him to see what she sees.

He follows her gaze. "Ça alors," he says, studying the façade. "And those vines spilling from the broken windowpanes. It is beautiful in a way, is it not?"

Ester nods, and her slight frame sways with the breeze. Jules cradles her arm, lest she falls.

"Many times I have wondered how she would look," she says, "but never did I imagine new life taking root within these walls. Look how Mara nourishes and cares for them."

Jules shifts his weight, unsure how he should respond. She speaks of the château as if it were a living person. As a child, his grand-mère told him stories about gargoyles. That they come alive at night and speak to humans when wind passes through their mouths. But his grand-mère never believed these legends. Not truly. No matter what Ester imagines, castles are not alive. They're not. But Ester is rather convincing.

"There are five hundred of them," she says, turning to face him. "Windows, that is. And a hundred rooms—I counted them myself. Even found the secret ones."

"Ah, bon?" Jules raises an eyebrow. He's not just being polite. His curiosity is genuine. "And when was this?"

Tick. Tick. Tick.

Her pulse beats in her temples. "Long before the windows were broken, but many years after the Count fled." Ester knows her explanation isn't enough, but one detail will surely lead to another.

"The Count left her behind?" Jules clucks his tongue. "How can people abandon something so dear?"

"I have wondered the same," she whispers. "Every child did." Ester stays quiet while the past crumbles around her. "You know this was an orphanage, oui?"

Jules' face slackens. Mon Dieu. He now understands why they are here.

"During the war?" he asks.

She shakes her head. "It was used as barracks until the war ended."

"German troops?" Jules gazes at the shallow relief carvings around the arched entrance.

"Non," she says, staring at him with her pale blue eyes. "Allied soldiers fighting battles nearby."

From the corner of her eye, Ester glimpses curtains billowing in the summer breeze, but she doesn't turn her head lest they vanish. Not even when children laugh in the distance, splashing in the enormous marble fountain they had once used as a wading pool. Ester studies the green and gold flecks in Jules' irises as dozens of girls cheer and shriek on the manicured lawn. Linking arms, they form a long serpentine chain and move as a single entity—like the coiled tail of a dragon. And there, among the smiling scrubbed faces, is Esterbell. She's wearing a cotton summer dress with bobby socks and saddle shoes, and a pale yellow ribbon in her dark hair.

"Madame Bell?" Jules touches her shoulder, rousing her from her trance-like state.

Ester blinks and glances around. The children have vanished, taking the sunshine with them. She turns back to Mara, and she's dark and hollow again. Both of them.

"Call me Ester." She takes a moment to clear her head. "In a few days, Mara will be demolished. Reduced to a pile of rubble. I didn't grow up in a house with parents or siblings—not blood relations. This is my childhood."

He thinks of the stone farmhouse where his grand-mère raised him. How it now sits empty.

"Je suis désolé. How long did you live here?" The thought of her never being adopted weighs on his chest like a heavy stone. But he's invested. He must know.

"I left when I was eighteen. It was agonizing after living here for so long. I thought there would always be a road home, but now Mara is leaving *me* and taking my past with her."

"C'est tellement triste," he says. The words come out tinny. Trite. Perhaps if he weren't working, he could tell Ester he knows the sting of being left behind. He'd explain his father left before he was born, and his mother left a few years after. He'd tell her his grand-mère raised him, and he's better off because of it. He knows he is. But the hollow ache is still there. It never leaves him. Why can't his wife understand this? Perhaps because he never explained it well enough. Perhaps those long conversations were only in his head.

This should have been a simple half-day assignment for Jules. Drive a nice old woman to the countryside to see a château, then drive her back to the city. But now, here he is. His head is throbbing, and his limbs are heavy like he's been hiking for weeks. He wasn't even on the schedule today. If Gaspard wasn't ill, Jules would be back at his flat, watching the match and ironing shirts. But he wouldn't have met Ester.

Tick. Tick. Tick.

"Have you ever lived in the past?" she asks, searching his face.

Jules blinks a few times and rubs his eye, trying to clear away a bit of debris. Is it dust? A stray eyelash? Clients never ask personal questions. They like talking about themselves. Breakups, affairs, family quarrels over money. It's easy to share secrets from the backseat of a dark Mercedes. Ester has been open with him. She's shared private stories, answered his nosy questions. And yet Jules is hesitant to share his grief. How many times has his wife complained about this very thing? This is why his marriage failed. He knows it's true. But it's taking an eccentric old woman and a dying castle for him to see it.

"Oui," he says. "A bottle of Bordeaux always helps." He stares up at the clock tower. "But I'm always back by morning."

Ester smiles, but she's distracted now. The cogs are turning.

"Jules?" she says. "Could it be that the past trails after us? That it's not something we can leave behind?" She turns her gaze to the dark portico. "Perhaps the past is like a shadow. Though close, only the outline is visible."

"My wife and I separated, and she wants a divorce." The words shoot out like a tightly coiled spring—a spring he thought permanently stuck. But even so, what is he thinking? He has told *no one*, let alone a client. Sure, Gaspard knows. He guessed the morning Jules signed the lease on his flat. Gaspard took one look at him and knew.

Did Ester hear him? Jules wants to take back his words, so he can relax and be safe again.

"Sometimes the past does feel like a shadow," he continues. "I only wish we could choose which versions of our past may tag along."

"Perhaps you can find your way back to her," she says. The sky dims, and she stares up at the swollen rain clouds that blanket the castle.

"I don't think there *is* a way back for me." Heat rises in his cheeks. "We want different things."

"What is it you want?" she says, not missing a beat. The afternoon murk has done away with niceties.

The pink blush reaches the tips of Jules' ears. He shrugs like a schoolboy—like his teacher has called on him, and he's caught without an answer.

"Your wife, then?" she adds. "What does *she* want?"

His face blooms red.

"A child." He stares at his leather shoes, tracing a line of stitching.

Ester is quiet for a long moment.

"And you're certain you don't want the same?" she says.

"I thought I was." He takes off his cap and rakes his fingers through his hair, trying to ease the pressure in his head.

"Does she know you're uncertain?"

"Non. I've been quite adamant. I never knew my father, and I barely remember my mother. My grand-mère raised me." He speaks as if this explains everything. And maybe it does.

"Siblings?" she asks.

His face slackens. "I would have liked that."

Ester closes her eyes, and the images appear one after another.

"The orphanage had barely been open a year when I arrived in 1946. There were fifty-eight children living here."

"That's quite a lot," he says. "What did you think about Mara?"

She opens her eyes when he calls Mara by name. "I was six. The details are hazy. But it was a troubling time, as you'd expect." She takes his arm again. It's comforting. "Like you, I didn't have brothers or sisters, but many who arrived with their siblings were later split apart. Just as they were forming a new outer shell." Her eyes are wet. "I saw what they went through. The second wave of grief was too much. It haunted them."

"Did the children know why they were here?"

She thinks for a moment. "Some did. The older ones, mainly. For many of us, there were no answers. There will never be." She tucks a strand of fine white hair behind her ears. "The war created many orphans. Sometimes for reasons we don't talk about."

Jules flips back through old history lessons. "I've heard things. But never in school."

She grips the smooth wooden handle of her walking stick.

"Non, that wouldn't happen. Those babies were forbidden. Still not discussed, even today." Ester's cheeks flush. "Two hundred thousand babies were born to French women who'd mingled with occupying German soldiers. Their babies were considered a betrayal to the country. Terrible mistakes. The mothers lived in shame their entire lives. The children were taunted throughout childhood."

He sucks in his breath. "C'est terrible. No baby is a mistake."

Ester pats his arm, wanting his words to sink in.

"Of course, children were orphaned for other reasons. Even one parent dying was enough to lose one's family." She glances up at the saplings growing under impossible conditions and marvels at their bravery. "The war left many young widows unable to feed all their children. And so, they sent some away. Sacrificed, so their brothers and sisters could stay." She spots a shadowy stream of smoke rising from a chimney at the back of the castle. "But here I am, going on and on."

"No, please continue."

"The question you asked about Mara." Ester gazes up at a spiraling tower in the east wing and points to a broken window. "My first bedroom was just up there. A half-dozen girls shared the room—two of whom became close friends. It was a difficult first year, but the château was a lively place, and I was mostly all right during the day. They kept us busy with school lessons and meals. A few light chores. Plenty of time to play. In the daylight hours, laughter echoed through the halls, and our smiles comforted one another." Ester folds her arms as if trying to hold herself together. She focuses on the swirling smoke still rising from the chimney. "At night, when we slipped back into our memories, the ache returned. Every child had a different story, and Mara listened to them all. As she cradled us in her quiet calm, she drew our sorrow into these walls.

"Each passing year was a bit easier. We coped in our own ways. When I grew older—twelve, maybe?—I wandered the hallways while everyone slept. By then, my room was on the back side of the château, and it was easier to sneak out. If the other girls knew, they never said. Every fortnight, I slipped out of the room at midnight, teetering on the threshold between day and night—between past and present. I climbed twisting spiral staircases, crossed long corridors—from east to west, north to south—and descended heavy stone steps that drowned my footfall. Being on a hilltop, we had the most violent storms. Buckets of rain. Rolling thunder. Lightning so bright, it lit up a room like a bolt of daylight. This was my favorite time to wander.

"At fourteen, I grew daring. I took the staircase up to the clock tower—off-limits, of course—and climbed a tiny, coiled staircase to the tower roof. From there, I could crawl into the clock chamber. Oh, it was black as pitch up there. I had only a small oil lamp I kept on my night table. But inside the clock chamber, I felt closer to Mara."

"Did you tell anyone?" Jules stares up at the tower, trying to imagine her tucked away in the chamber.

"Not until now," she says, still holding his arm. "On another of my ramblings, I found a secret staircase that led me to a cellar. I discovered a room strewn with old war letters and official-type papers. And when I was a bit older, I found a folding staircase in a ceiling—a pull-down ladder—and climbed up to a large attic flat filled with dust and mildew. No one had lived there for some time, but the flat was still well-furnished with a grand four-poster bed, a lady's dressing table, and an elegant desk filled with love letters. I read them all by lamplight." She meets Jules' eyes. "There were always new places to explore. A new route I hadn't yet taken. A door I had yet to open."

"I don't think I was ever that brave," he says, shaking his head. "To roam the belly of the dragon alone. Was it not frightening?"

Ester turns and studies his face. "My parents left me and never returned. What would be worse than that?"

He glances down at his shoes again and says nothing. There's nothing to say.

"When I wandered at night, I was lighter," she says, patting his arm. "That constant ache for the past subsided, if only for a while. By sixteen, my earliest memories were blurred and fragmented, like pieces of a dream. I wanted to leave them behind so I could leave the pain behind, but if I let the memories float away, I would have no past at all. That frightened me even more." She falls silent.

"I'm not sure if your children live nearby," Jules says, "but if you mean to have time alone with Mara, I believe I'm intruding."

Ester glances up as though she's forgotten he's there.

"I don't have children," she whispers.

He frowns. This isn't the answer he expected. She's longed for a family. Why not start one of her own? But when his words echo in his head, he knows it's not as easy as that.

"You're surprised," Ester says, giving him a half-smile. "Everyone was. Especially when I didn't marry. I regret it though, to be honest. I don't believe I've told anyone that until now."

"Sorry to hear it." Jules knows the weight of regret. "But why not marry?"

She shrugs. "I would be expected to have children. If not by the man, then his mother. The first time a man proposed to me, I said I didn't plan on having a child. It did not go well. Thereafter, I told suitors I wasn't ready—that I intended to buy the boutique de chocolat where I had worked since leaving the château. And that's what I did. The original owner allowed me to live in the cramped flat above the boutique, and I saved my money until he was ready to sell." She gazes at the dark portico. "But there was another reason I didn't marry. Something I did not understand until later."

"What's that?" he says.

"When I was an orphan, no one chose me. So, I chose myself."

Without another word, Ester walks to the lancet-arched front door set in the hollow of the portico. Jules' pulse quickens. Is she thinking of going inside? It's not safe. He follows and waits under the stone-arch where the gargoyle peers down at him, ready to pounce. Jules is far enough to give Ester privacy, but close enough to reach her in three long strides.

She stands before the deep intricate carvings on the front door, touching the wood as if it were a contoured map. Her fingertips follow every ridge and hollow of a dragon rising high above the forest clearing. She traces the sharp, jagged fangs, a massive mouth, and a long, curved neck. The prickly spikes that run the length of the dragon's spine, and an enormous pair of wings. Her hand pauses when she reaches the smaller dragon breaking through the forest canopy, trailing after its elder, learning how to soar through the clouds. How to reach the heavens.

Peering through the window, a sharp sound catches in her throat. Ester sees the wreckage strewn across the floor. The broken stone balustrades on the staircase. The shattered marble steps. Her gaze floats up to the vaulted ceiling, to the vivid colors of her childhood, but the pastel hues have long since paled. Ester rests her head against the filthy windowpane and closes her eyes. Her breaths come shallow, like Mara's.

Tick. Tick. Tick.

Concerned, Jules walks to the window and stands at her side. Through the grimy glass, he spots crumbling walls, rotten floorboards, a partially collapsed ceiling—the château is in ruins. It's worse than he imagined. But he takes a closer look. He tries to see the room through Ester's eyes—to see how it looked when she had been a child of the castle. Jules catches a glimpse of the château's former splendor, and his stomach flutters. Even in her broken state, Mara is captivating.

"Jules?" Ester stands up straight, hands trembling. "Would you be kind enough to bring me something from the car?"

Deep creases cut into his brow. "Oui," he says, but he hesitates. "What is it you need?"

Ester pauses too long. "My yellow headscarf."

He rubs his forehead, trying to fit the puzzle pieces together. He doesn't recall seeing a yellow scarf.

"How about we walk back to the car together?" he says, offering his hand.

"I'm afraid I'm not ready." She doesn't meet his eyes.

Jules' feet are rooted to the ground.

"I'll be all right," she says. "I have my walking stick."

He hears the pleading in her voice. Something isn't right. He knows it. But how can he refuse? The car isn't very far. He'll be quick.

"Alright," he says, passing under the gargoyle. "I'll only be a moment."

"Jules?" Ester raises her voice over the wind. "I'm glad it was you who drove me today." Her pale blue eyes are glossy, but she's smiling.

"It is my pleasure, Madame." Her words make him lighter. It takes all his willpower not to break into a jog.

The roar of his heartbeat fills his ears as he throws open the back door of the sedan. He checks the seat—no scarf. He scans the floor—nothing. Did it get pushed underneath? Jules crouches down to search under the seat, and a heavy door slams shut. The sound makes his stomach fall away.

Jules leaps up and hits his head on the ceiling, knocking off his cap. He rushes back to the dark hollow, but when he reaches the front door, she's gone. Her walking stick is propped up against the stone wall, but Ester is gone.

The broken stairs, the smashed-up floor, the half-collapsed ceiling—what if she falls? What if the ceiling caves in? Jules pushes the bronze lever and bursts through the front door, but he stops on the threshold. The walls, the ceiling, the ornate staircase—nothing is damaged. Everything is perfectly intact.

A young girl rounds the corner, eyes sparkling.

"See? I told you I'd be all right." The girl is wearing a plain cotton dress, scuffed saddle shoes, and a lemon chiffon ribbon on account of her being seven years old.

Jules steps closer. He studies her pale blue eyes and her dark hair. Her heart-shaped face.

"Ester?"

The girl smiles. "Esterbell."

Inside Jules, a wall crumbles. He doesn't stop the tears. He can't.

"Why?" His voice cracks.

"I want another turn." Esterbell's voice is sunlight. "This time I can choose anything I want and not be worried like before. I know there's nothing to be afraid of."

Jules crouches down, and she hugs him around the neck like it's the most natural thing in the world.

"Don't be sad." Her voice is thick and shaky. "If I grow old again, I'll get to see you."

"I'd like that," he says, blinking back tears. He keeps hugging her. She hasn't let him go. "You're an incredible person, Esterbell. As a mother or a daughter, I would certainly choose you."

She pulls back to see his face—to see if he means it. Esterbell grins, eyes bright with tears.

"Talk to your wife and tell her things, so you can go home," she says. "You'll be a great papa."

Jules lowers his head.

"Don't be worried. Be brave like me!" Her cheeks are rosy.

"You're right—I shall do that." He straightens his shoulders. "I'll be brave like you."

Esterbell wrinkles her forehead. "Even if you get scared?"

Jules imagines himself going home. His real home. "Even then."

It's time to say goodbye. They both know this.

She takes the lemon chiffon ribbon from her hair and drops it into his palm. "I do hope you have a daughter someday."

Jules nods. "Perhaps I will name her Esterbell."

A chime of voices drift down the marble staircase. Esterbell turns her head, ears perked, and hears the tap-tap-tapping of saddle-shoes. A grin lights up her face.

"Those are my friends," she whispers, turning back to Jules.

He smiles. "Go be with them." He keeps his voice steady, for her sake.

She furrows her brow. "But I don't want to say goodbye."

He tries to swallow the lump in his throat.

"Remember what you said?" he asks. "One day you'll grow old, and—"

"And I'll see you again!" she says with a little hop.

Esterbell gives him one last hug and walks to the staircase, dragging her feet. Holding the smooth wooden banister, she leaps onto the first step and glances over her shoulder to see Jules standing at the front door. His hand is on the shiny bronze lever, and her lemon chiffon ribbon peeks out from his breast coat pocket. Esterbell waves, her eyes full of doubt. She doesn't move from her spot. But then Jules gives her a smile and his eyes light up, and she finds the courage to soar. Like a young dragon rising from the forest floor, Esterbell darts up the towering staircase and breaks through the clouds.

As the castle door closes, the latch clicks, and the gears of time rewind.

THE TWO LIVES OF AGAPITO CORTEZ

Carlos Joaquin Gonzalez

Agapito's ears rang from the thunder of cannon fire. His skin was clammy and hot, the chills wouldn't stop, and the pain—his left arm was on fire, torn to shreds by Confederate bullets.

The blood-soaked bandage on Agapito's arm needed to be changed. The infection was getting worse—he knew it—but he couldn't bear to look. Not yet. Agapito closed his eyes, wanting it all to go away. The open wound, the fever, the ringing in his ears. He had been there for days, and a doctor still hadn't treated him. Not properly. He was alone, forgotten in the heat of battle, drifting in and out of consciousness as sepsis set in.

He'd been unlucky. They'd placed Agapito in a field hospital lost to the Rebels during the battle. The doctor in charge of treating him and a dozen other patients had been captured and used as leverage. One of the many prisoner swaps that came with battles of this magnitude. And so, Agapito Cortez languished for another day. He would not be rescued. He lay waiting to die.

By the time Union soldiers reached the field hospital, Agapito was the only patient with a pulse. The others had bled out or died of infection days before.

"Jesus Christ." The Union officer held his nose as he approached the cot. Agapito was no more than a husk, drawing his last breaths. "I'm sorry we couldn't get here sooner." The officer spoke in a soothing voice used for dying soldiers.

Agapito did not reply. There was nothing to say to the blurry figure in front of him, delivering his last rites. His eyes closed, and his breathing slowed. Agapito revisited the early years of his childhood with his father, mother, and sisters. Memories of his life before soldiers had destroyed the family ranch during the Mexican American War.

His life would've been so different had he grown up with his family. If he hadn't spent thirteen years in the orphanage. If he had made different choices at eighteen. He regretted ever leaving Mexico. But there had been nothing left for him. No one left for him.

Agapito had traveled from the state of Tamaulipas to Kansas because a shady childhood friend had promised him work. He had packed all his possessions into a canvas bag: two changes of clothes, a shaving kit, a canteen, and a small, creased photograph of his parents that was taken by a traveling photographer months before they died. But there was no job waiting for him in Kansas. And he didn't have money to return to Mexico. So Agapito stayed in the United States—a country he hated. The country that had killed his family.

In Kansas, there had been recruiters on every corner. The confederates had attacked Fort Sumter, and the U.S. military was scrambling to raise an army. As a Mexican national, they could not conscript Agapito, but he needed money to survive. He let go of his hatred and joined the Union army, deciding the United States was the lesser of two evils.

During his four years at war, Agapito had never given much thought to his mission, his country, or his enemy. He'd solely focused on his fellow soldiers and the companionship they offered. Those nights around the campfire brought him solace. They were the family he needed. Near the end of the war, Agapito's regiment was deployed to Texas. On May 12th, 1865, he had fought fiercely against the Rebels in the Battle of Palmito Hill.

The memories stopped, and the voice of a young woman beckoned Agapito.

He opened his eyes and gazed at the woman who sat at his bedside. She had a kind face, with warm eyes and long dark lashes. A rich brown complexion, and two black braids that cascaded down her back. The nurse reminded Agapito of the young Indian woman who'd made tortillas stuffed with huitlacoche when he was a boy. His favorite food.

"Ay, gracias a Dios," the nurse said, wringing her hands. "You're finally awake."

Agapito glanced around a small hospital room filled with morning sun. Every bed was full. The soldiers were alive. And the blood-splattered white flaps of the hospital tent were gone. In their place were yellow adobe brick walls reminiscent of his childhood.

"I've been transferred," he whispered, voice thick with emotion. Someone had taken care of him. He sat up and put his weight on his left arm without thinking, and his stomach sank. There was no bandage on his arm. No red streaks, no open wound. Not even a scar.

"My wound," he said, glancing up at the nurse. "How long have I been here?"

"Since yesterday," she said, smiling softly. "I was here when they brought you from the field. My name is Tiburcia." She lifted his wrist and took his pulse. "Do you remember arriving?"

Agapito shook his head. The room smelled like iodine and metal—like blood.

"Imanol? Do you remember him?" There was a gentleness in her voice.

Agapito sat up straight. He didn't remember.

"Do you know your name?" Tiburcia furrowed her brow. "Do you remember the battle?"

"Agapito Cortez," he whispered. "It was the Battle at Palmito Hill. I was on the front lines."

"You were fighting at Boca Chica," she said, frowning.

"Boca Chica?" Agapito shook his head. He knew the fog of war—he'd seen it in other soldiers. But his memories were clear. "No," he said, "it was Palmito Hill. I was shot in the arm." He rubbed his bicep. "Someone dragged me to the hospital tent. I don't know who." He sat back. Beads of sweat formed along his hairline. "I don't know how long I was there. I was dying."

"You mean *here*." Tiburcia touched the back of her hand to his forehead.

Agapito stared at a soft bundle of clothing at the foot of his bed.

"The Rebels came and took the doctor prisoner," he said. "I was the only patient still alive. I was left behind, alone."

"You're not alone anymore," she said, squeezing his hand.

A man wearing a blood-streaked white coat strode towards them. He had fierce green eyes and a red beard.

"Why are you still here, Cortez?" The doctor said, flipping through his chart.

The only answer Agapito had was the truth.

"I had sepsis," Agapito said. "I was shot in the arm, and—"

Tiburcia nudged his foot.

"Dios mio!" The doctor nearly spat his words. "Listen to your Indian gibberish." The doctor's Spanish accent was unfamiliar. It was as if he'd declared war on the letters *s* and *z*. "How ungrateful you Indians are." He shot Agapito and Tiburcia dark glances. "Do not forget you are subjects of the Crown."

"Si, of course," Tiburcia said, lowering her eyes. She nudged Agapito again.

Agapito didn't bother explaining he was mestizo.

"We have two soldiers arriving," the doctor said, "and unlike *yourself*, they're badly wounded."

"He might have a concussion," Tiburcia said in a small voice. "He has false memories."

The doctor turned to the nurse. "*Go*—both of you! Get him out of my sight."

"I'm still on duty," Tiburcia said, wringing her hands. She glanced up at the clock—8:00 a.m. "I have two hours left."

"Your shift is over," the doctor said, scribbling furiously. He didn't bother glancing up.

When the doctor moved on to the next patient, Tiburcia handed Agapito the bundle of clothes at the foot of the bed.

"These aren't my clothes," he said, unfolding the bundle.

Gone was his black felt Hardee hat, his Prussian blue wool coat, and the sky-blue trousers issued by the United States army. In its place was a blue-and-white striped guayabera tunic with four large cargo pockets, matching rayadillo trousers, and a straw hat. Tiburcia turned her back to give him privacy, and Agapito slipped into the pair of soft cotton pants.

"Are these supposed to be loose?" he said, tying the drawstring.

"Si," Tiburcia said, "just get dressed."

Agapito quickly laced up his shoes and slid his arms into the tunic.

"Where's my bag?" he said, fastening the hook and eye closure on his standing collar.

"What bag?"

"My shoulder bag!" Agapito's heart was racing. He searched around the cot, kneeled, peered underneath. "Where is it?"

"Shh. You didn't have one." Tiburcia picked up his hat.

Agapito sat back on his heels. He was sweating, his dark brown hair plastered to his forehead. "It's gone," he whispered to himself. The portrait of his parents was lost forever.

Tiburcia hooked his arm, pulled him to his feet, and led him to the exit. When they reached the dented metal door set in adobe brick, Agapito stopped. It was a far cry from the white flaps of the medical tent. He didn't know what he'd find on the other side. Hands trembling, he pushed the rusted lever and crossed the threshold.

On the other side of the door was a bustling street. Shielding his face from the sun, Agapito peered around, finding the landscape both alien and familiar. Street vendors stood on every corner, selling tamales, tacos, and chicharrones. Ceramic tile roofs topped rows of pastel-colored shops and houses. A priest led a group of Indian monks to the mission to pray for the wounded.

But what caught Agapito's attention most was a young newsboy, maybe ten years old.

"Extra, extra! Consiga tu periodico!" the newsboy cried. "American President Breckinridge assassinated at last! Yankee morale at an all-time low!"

"Breckinridge lost to Lincoln," Agapito said, approaching the newsboy. "He's no president!"

The newsboy took a step back.

"How much?" Agapito fumbled through his pockets, searching for money. "What do you take around here? Pesos? Dollars?"

"I don't know what a peso is, Señor." The boy lifted his cap and scratched his head. "And I sure don't take dollars." He held out his waiting palm. "Dos reales."

Tiburcia brushed past Agapito and gave the boy three coins. "Keep the change, muchacho."

"Muchas gracias, Señorita Tiburcia!"

Tiburcia gave Agapito his hat and led him away from the crowd before handing him the newspaper. He quickly scanned the first page.

Periodico Las Palomas
13 de Mayo, 1865 Anno Domini

Breckinridge Dead! Yankee defeat Imminent!

On May 12[Th] we first reported the assassination of American President John C. Breckinridge by Spanish sympathizer John Patrick Riley during a showing of "Our American Cousin" at Ford's Theater. Señor Riley, a veteran of the Empire's St. Patrick's Battalion, yelled, "Ad Majorem Dei Gloriam"—for the greater glory of God—as he jumped from the viewing balcony. These were his last words. Yankee soldiers later murdered him in cold blood. This act of justice follows decades of mistreatment of our Irish Catholic brothers and sisters by...

Nausea rose to the back of Agapito's throat. Everything was wrong. All of it.

"Come sit down." Tiburcia led him to a nearby bench. Her exasperated look was the same one his mother had given him whenever he came home late from a day of exploring the chaparral. Agapito sat next to Tiburcia and read the next headline.

A Holy Roman Empire for the modern era: How the Nation of Charlemagne has rapidly industrialized.

He flipped frantically through the pages of the newspaper, struggling to catch his breath.

The hunt for Simon Bolivar: Meet the Crown's Brave soldiers hot on the trail of this Senile Insurrectionist.

He searched for anything he might recognize—anything to reassure him the world he knew still existed.

Rumblings in the north: Who are the Indians of the Ghost Dance Movement?

After reading the newspaper inside and out, Agapito was lightheaded.

"What is it?" Tiburcia asked, laying her hand on his forearm.

"I'm not *from* here." The newspaper trembled in his hands.

"Are you a settler from the Northern Territories?" she asked.

"Northern Territories?" He rubbed his face. "Tiburcia, please listen. I am a Union soldier. I was wounded at the Battle of Palmito Hill, and I need to get back to my regiment."

"Which Union do you fight to protect?"

"Which Union?" he said. "The United States of America. The thirty-four states!" He needed her to believe him. To understand. "I've been fighting against the Confederacy since they seceded from the Union."

"Ay, Dios mio." She covered her mouth. "The United States has nineteen states."

"Look—I think I died in a field tent. This isn't my world."

A young man came running towards them, yelling Agapito's name. His uniform was similar, but this man was an officer, and their features couldn't be more different. He had light blue eyes, blond hair, and white skin that made alarm bells sound in Agapito's head.

"Aspaldiko! Zer moduz, Cortez?" the young man called out.

Agapito took a step back. The man wasn't speaking Spanish. And it wasn't an Indian language he'd ever heard.

"What's he saying?" Agapito whispered to Tiburcia. "What language is that?"

"Basque," she whispered back. "Growing up in Nueva Orleans, I heard it often."

The man caught up to them.

"Have you forgotten the Basque I taught you?" he said, clapping Agapito on the back.

Agapito studied his face. There was nothing familiar about him.

"I'm glad you're feeling better." the young man said. "I wanted to stay with you until you woke, but the doctor kicked me out."

"Imanol was worried about you," Tiburcia said, pressing her fingertips against Agapito's back.

Imanol turned to Tiburcia. "Ah! You're the nurse who cared for him when I brought him in."

Tiburcia forced a smile. "Si. Will you excuse us for one moment?" She took Agapito's hand and led him several feet away. Her skin was so warm, so nurturing.

"Who is he?" Agapito said, not letting go of her hand.

"You don't recognize Imanol Iparralde? He's a war hero. He

brought you to the hospital during the battle and introduced himself as your best friend."

"My best friend?" Agapito swallowed hard. He hadn't had a best friend since he had lived at the orphanage. He'd cried over her for months after she was adopted. "I've never met him before."

Tiburcia scrunched up her face as though she didn't know what to believe.

"Well, he cares about you," she said. "Just go along with it for now." Still holding his hand, she led him back to Imanol. "Please don't think us rude," she said, "you've done so much for Agapito. But he's still struggling. It's not been an easy recovery."

"I'm glad I found you, Cortez. Some angry Spanish doctor barked at me, saying you'd left an hour ago. I was running around looking for you until the newsboy pointed me in the right direction."

Tiburcia glanced down the street. "Can we get out of the sun?"

Imanol mopped his brow and nodded. "We'll go to my house, Agapito. You can stay there."

"You want me to stay with you?" Agapito wrinkled his forehead.

"Haven't I convinced you?" Imanol turned to Tiburcia. "My parents bought a house here not long ago. They've finally accepted I'll be based here in Las Palomas for a while." He clapped Agapito on the back again. "You'll be happy to know I took your bag there for safekeeping."

"My bag?" Agapito wondered whose bag it was—it couldn't be his. "Gracias, Emmanuel."

"Since when do you use my Spanish name?" Imanol laughed and slapped him on the shoulder again.

Agapito searched Tiburcia's eyes, not wanting to say goodbye. He didn't know her well, but he knew her more than the Imanol guy. And with her, he didn't have to pretend.

"Will you come with us?" Agapito asked her. "So, you'll know where I'll be staying?"

Tiburcia's cheeks turned deep red. "I guess I can come for a short time," she said. "I'll be expected home in a couple of hours."

Agapito's heart sank. Of course, someone would be expecting her.

"I live in a boarding house with the other nurses," she said as if reading his expression. "They'll wonder where I am. My real home is hours away, in Nueva Orleans."

Agapito relaxed his shoulders. They followed Imanol down the wide cobblestone street to a plaza anchored by a Gothic limestone cathedral. The square was crowded with palmetto trees and flocks of gray doves, flapping and strutting, bobbing their heads as they pecked the ground for crumbs.

"Where did you live before joining el Ejército de Tierra?" Tiburcia asked Imanol.

"I'm from a sleepy trading post in Nueva California."

"Where?" she asked.

"It's called Las Vegas. You've probably never heard of it—it's a tiny place. We're known for our freshwater springs," Imanol said. "My family's been there for two generations. We're originally from Nafarroa, in Basque Country."

Agapito stayed quiet, hoping he wasn't expected to know any details of Imanol's life.

They passed the west nave of the cathedral. Agapito stopped and craned his neck, staring up at the stained-glass petals of the rose window. Imanol waved them across the road and ushered them down a winding side street with uneven cobblestones. They passed row after row of pastel-colored houses.

"I can't complain. My family has done well in Nueva California,"

Imanol said, "but I wanted something different, so I joined the army. I was too young—sixteen—but I lied about my age."

"That *is* young," Tiburcia said. "And you've come so far."

"After eight years of service and a bit of luck," Imanol said.

Sure. Luck, Agapito thought. If being lucky meant having white skin.

"And now you're a war hero," Tiburcia said, smiling.

"No more than other soldiers defending the Crown," Imanol said, shrugging. "I know a guy from Nuevo Santander who's saved my life many times." He smiled and gestured to Agapito. "Si, Cortez? How many battles have we fought against the Yankees?"

"Too many." Agapito forced a smile.

Agapito first thought Tiburcia was only being polite. Or maybe asking questions for his own sake, to help jog his memory. But she sounded so interested in Imanol. It made sense, though. The guy was handsome, he had money, he had his own house. And he belonged in this world, like Tiburcia. Agapito felt his connection to her slipping away.

Finally, they reached Imanol's home and followed him inside. The house smelled of fragrant Far East spices and the lingering scent of pintxos. Imanol said he ate them daily, as they reminded him of his mother and his roots.

"Make yourself at home," Imanol said, leading them into the parlor.

Home. The word stung Agapito. His last real home was a lifetime ago. Tiburcia and Agapito settled on the velvet couch, and Imanol went into the kitchen to make café con leches. When he returned, he placed a wide canvas bag against the couch, and Agapito eyed it warily. It was similar in shape, but it was not his bag.

"I've been wanting to ask you," Imanol said. "Do you remember what happened on the battlefield?" Imanol took a sip of his coffee.

Agapito shook his head, relieved he didn't have to lie. That part was true.

"The running? The explosion?" Imanol sighed and set his mug on the coffee table. "I didn't see it happen—you were on the ground when I found you. I thought you were dead. When I reached your side, there was no blood. You were unconscious but breathing. Everyone around you had died."

"I remember waking up in the field tent," Agapito said.

"Tent?" Imanol raised his eyebrows.

"Hospital, I mean."

Imanol sat back in his chair. He was quiet for a moment. "You don't seem like yourself, Cortez."

Agapito shot Tiburcia a look. When the doctor had questioned him, she had nudged him before he had said too much, but now she just shrugged. If she trusted Imanol, maybe he should trust him too.

"There's something I should tell you both," Agapito said.

And with that, he told them about the bullets and the infection. How he'd been abandoned. How he had died. And then he told them everything he could about the civil war and the events leading up to it. When he finished, he sat quietly, waiting for one of them to speak.

"If I am to believe what you've explained," Imanol said, dragging out his words, "the dividing point seems to be this Mexican War of Independence—The Indian Uprising, as we call it." Imanol's face reddened. He glanced at Tiburcia, but she did not meet his eyes.

"But how could the Crown let its Empire crumble?" Tiburcia asked Agapito.

"Because there was no Crown at the time," he explained.

"Napoleon invaded Spain, leaving the colonies without backup. With the Spanish rulers vulnerable, people from all races and classes came together and defeated the Spaniards across the Empire."

"But Spain was never invaded." Imanol rubbed his face. "I've never heard of a man called Napoleon or these Napoleonic wars you spoke of." He paused. "But there *were* reforms in the 1820s that narrowly defeated the insurrectionist uprisings across the Empire. That's when the Crown took a hard look at itself and decided it was time to adapt. They needed a more reciprocal model of governing—like how the British rule their colonies. They finally understood their model of taking from the colonies was unsustainable, and no one dared to disagree. Be it royal court or government official, anyone who questioned the Crown was executed on the spot."

Agapito stared over Imanol's shoulder. Those same events *could* have happened in his world. But they didn't.

"My father used to talk about the ten years of peace from 1820 to 1830," Tiburcia said. "In Nueva Orleans, they removed the entire government from power and replaced them with reformist politicians. And eventually, everyone forgot the revolution had ever happened. Except for radical holdouts like Simon Bolivar." She shook her head. "At eighty-one years old, he's still in the jungles of South America, fighting the Spanish in a dead-end guerilla war."

"Si," Imanol said. "The 1830s are when things got bad again. The United States fell under the spell of manifest destiny." He rolled his eyes. "They believed God chose *them* to unite the country from el Atlántico to el Pacifico, and they attacked the Empire's borders. Still recovering from the uprisings and reforms, the Crown let the incursions slide."

"They did nothing?" Agapito said.

"Not until...what? 1846?" Imanol said. "That's when a military expedition plunged far into the New Spanish interior. They attacked San Antonio, finally forcing the Spanish Empire into a war with the United States. While the Spanish Empire was sizable, the Yankees had their technology and tactics, so it was a stalemate for a long time. It wasn't until five years ago that Spain used all its resources to hold the line at the border."

"And the rest of the world?" Agapito said, scooting to the edge of the couch.

Imanol shrugged and thought for a moment.

"Other European kingdoms took notice of our resolve," Imanol said. "They rescinded their support of the Yankees. And our Viceroy was ingenious. He secured non-aggression treaties with Indian tribes of the Northern Territories and covertly funded slave rebellions across the American south." Imanol clapped his hands together. "So, with their president dead, it's only a matter of time before the Yankees capitulate. But later, I think men will look back on the Spanish victory as a pyrrhic one. We've lost far more men than the Yankees."

A sense of calm washed over Agapito. He finally understood the world he was in.

"But enough of that," Imanol said with a smile. "I have good news for you. They have granted us leave."

"For what?" Agapito asked.

"Heroic acts and injuries."

Agapito bit the inside of his cheek. "I don't even know where I would go."

"To see your family, of course!" Imanol said.

"They're dead." Agapito stared down at his cup of coffee, warm in his hands. "They died seventeen years ago."

37

Imanol got up from his chair and put his arm around Agapito as only a best friend would.

"Every time you go on leave, you visit your family," Imanol said, softly. "Every night around the fire, you tell me how much you miss them. How you can't wait to see them again."

Agapito studied his face, not knowing what to believe.

"Hell, two years ago, I traveled with you to your family's ranch in Nuevo Santander and met them. They're alive, Cortez. Just last week your father sent you a postcard."

Agapito sunk into the back of the couch, tears streaming down his cheeks. Tiburcia wrapped her arms around his shoulders as if comforting a widow of a fallen soldier. But for Agapito, it was the opposite. His family was *alive*. They were far away, but maybe he could reach them.

In their silence, the tick of the clock grew louder. When Agapito caught his breath, he hoisted the canvas bag onto his lap. With trembling hands, he unbuttoned the flap and searched through the contents: a spare change of clothes; a bit of money; a bundle of letters from his family; and a small, creased photograph of his parents.

He dried his cheek with the back of his hand. He didn't have enough money, but the thought of waiting to see his family—it crushed him.

"I need to see them," he whispered, meeting Imanol's gaze. He had no memory of their past friendship, but already, Imanol had shown his compassion and generosity. "I have to get to Tamaulipas."

"Of course." A grin spread across Imanol's face, and he jumped up, full of energy. "The ranch where I board my horse isn't far, Cortez! If you wait here, I'll run down and saddle up Baboso. You can take him! That beast is fast, with endurance like I've never seen. I know you'll take good care of him."

"I can leave today?" Agapito spoke without a hint of emotion in his voice. Not because he didn't feel—because he felt too much. He'd never been happier or more scared in his life. It wasn't the trip that worried him—he'd grown up on a ranch, knew how to ride. There was a chance Imanol was wrong.

"It's not yet noon," Imanol said, checking the clock. "If I hurry, I can be back in a half-hour. You can make it to Villa Galeana by nightfall and stay with Pascual, like the last time we—" He stopped himself. "I know people down that way. Just remember that Tamaulipas is called Nuevo Santander, so use that name. People get suspicious, and you don't want any trouble." He put on his hat, and they followed him to the door.

"You're going to see your family, Cortez!" Imanol ran off down the road, leaving Agapito and Tiburcia to say their goodbyes.

For a moment, neither of them said a word.

"Tiburcia." Agapito took her hands in his. "It was you, wasn't it? Calling me into this world?"

"Not out loud," she said, blushing. "But I sat at your bedside while the other soldiers slept, if only for a few minutes. You had many bad dreams. I was worried. I wanted you to know I was there."

"Gracias," Agapito said. "When I saw you at my bedside, I knew I hadn't been alone." He pulled her close, breathing in the sweet scent of her hair. "The moment I get back, I will find you."

"You'd better keep your promise." Tiburcia laughed, but her eyes were glossy.

Agapito held her until he heard his best friend's voice. Such a great sound it was.

"Cortez!" Imanol yelled from outside. "Everything is ready for you, mi amigo!"

Agapito turned to Tiburcia and kissed her on the cheek. "I will keep my promise."

The two walked outside, and Imanol was standing next to Baboso, holding his reins.

"Vaya con Dios," Imanol said, embracing him. "Everything you need is in the saddlebag."

"Gracias for saving my life, Imanol. I owe you." Agapito turned to Tiburcia and hugged her tight. "I'll send you a telegram as soon as I can. Both of you." He climbed onto the saddle and took one last look at their smiling faces. "Gracias a los dos!" Agapito waved and trotted away. He missed them already.

"Buena suerte!" Imanol called out.

"Vuelve pronto a mi!" Tiburcia shouted.

And with that, Agapito rode off into the interior of New Spain to find the province of Nuevo Santander. To find his familia.

Agapito rode for hours without stopping and made it to Villa Galeana before dark. He found lodging with Imanol's friend, Pascual, slept soundly that night, and woke before daybreak the next morning. After feeding and watering Baboso, he saddled him up again, and they rode long after Agapito's canteens went dry.

Exhausted and dehydrated, Agapito's vision blurred. He was so close to his family's ranch, but without rest, he and Baboso would surely take a tumble. As much as he wanted to ride on, he stopped at a mission—a relic of the past. At least that's what he'd once thought. Agapito now saw missions as harbingers of the future. The unwilling union between Indian and Spaniard forged during the conquest would continue.

After tying up Baboso, Agapito fetched water and hay from an

Indian monk and headed for the mission proper, hoping to find food and water for himself. Just as he reached the mission doors, colorful fireworks rose from the center of town, blasting overhead. Agapito flinched, relaxing again as cheers erupted from passersby. It must be a local celebration, he decided. But deep down, he had a spark of hope.

Agapito heaved open the heavy wooden door and hurried down the cold, empty halls. When he reached the chapel, he found an old Indian man lying prostrate in front of the cross, praying in a language Agapito didn't understand.

"Excuse me, Señor," Agapito said, out of breath. "I'm traveling to see my family. I'm so close, but I can't go farther without food and water."

The old man stood—a priest.

"Welcome, my son," the priest said. "So beautiful it is to see young soldiers return to their families. Come with me. I'll find you something."

As they walked together, Agapito towered over the short priest and his lack of a tonsure; he had a full head of hair. And the priest's dark brown eyes, they seemed familiar. Eyes marred by a lifetime of sorrow.

The priest led Agapito to a rough-hewn table and disappeared into another room. Minutes later, he returned with two mugs of water and slices of bread with nata. With time to sit and think, hope bubbled inside Agapito's chest.

"The fireworks and the yelling," Agapito said. "Is it a local celebration?"

The priest's eyes met his. "It's the celebration you have hoped for," he said. "The one I have prayed for."

"The war is over," Agapito whispered to himself.

His mind spun in circles, wondering if he could stay with his family longer before returning to Las Palomas. But then he thought of Tiburcia and worried she'd go home to Nueva Orleans and he wouldn't see her again. And Imanol's horse! More than ever, he needed to send a telegram.

"How did the war end?" Agapito asked, spreading a thick layer of cream over the sweet bread.

"Diplomats from the United States met in Guadalupe Hidalgo today and signed a treaty, thus ending the war with the Spanish Empire. Regardless of who has won, the bloodshed is finally over."

"Have you lost family in the war?" Agapito took a bite of his bread.

"Had you understood Zapotec, you'd have heard me praying for freedom from all colonial powers wanting to control Mexico, be it American or Spanish. All Mexicanos are my family."

"Mexico," Agapito whispered. "On my journey, you're the first person I've met who's been brave enough to call it that."

"Mexico lives within us so long as we remember her name," said the priest. "It's a travesty. The Spanish sent Mexicanos to fight Americans—the same Americans that want to kill us for our land. The Spanish want our blood, and the Americans our soil. Either way, Mexico loses.

"When I was young, I dreamed of a Mexico I could claim as my own. I wanted to bring genuine change." The priest rested his head in his hands. "But in the Spaniard's New Spain, I am good for little. For this, my eyes are sad. When Mexico becomes free—and someday it shall—I will not be here to witness."

The fireworks sounded again in the distance, crying out like the voices of their ancestors waiting for a reply. Agapito stood and placed his hand on the priest's shoulder.

"They'll never know what could have been," he said to the priest. "Even with all of her flaws, Mexico, *my* Mexico, is a country worth fighting for."

The priest lifted his head and patted his hand.

"You never told me your name," Agapito said.

"You studied my face. Perhaps you already know me?" The priest smiled softly. "I am Father Benito Juarez."

Agapito knew him well. He understood the burden Father Juarez carried in his heart was the same burden carried by President Juarez—the man who had brought changes the priest only dreamed of.

"I wish you the best, Father," Agapito said, smiling. "It's an honor to have met you."

"The honor is mine," Father Juarez replied. "And the day our Mexico is free, you will hear my voice rise up with the fireworks."

Agapito rode off, buoyed by Father Juarez's hope that one day Mexico would be free, and men like himself would make the priest's dreams a reality. When Agapito reached the border of Nuevo Santander, another bloom of color exploded overhead. Although they went unspoken, Father Juarez's last words rang out in Zapotec and Latin, Nahua and Spanish. *Viva Mexico!* The words echoed in Agapito's soul.

May 15th, he thought, wanting to remember the day.

He was passing through the old fence that surrounded the farm proper when it struck him—it was his father's birthday. Agapito pushed Baboso faster, and as they galloped over the hill, he came upon a sight that flooded his body with warmth. Home. *His* home. A ranch surrounded by grain silos and endless pastures, untouched by war, or by time.

The air crackled with trumpets and guitars, and the breeze

carried the scent of mole and tamales. Agapito slid from his saddle and hitched his horse to the post, jogging the last hundred feet down the dirt path.

As he slipped through the rusted iron gate, his family's voices drifted out into the night as they sang *Las Mañanitas*. Shedding the sorrow he'd been carrying for years, Agapito slid the iron latch on the front door and ran into the arms of his parents.

THE THIRD QUIRK

Karin Larsen

I picked up the ship seven months after he died. He'd been float-ing near Rhem territory when the attack came. Apparently, it had taken the recovery crew three weeks to tow his broken vessel to the nearest space station for identification. From there, they'd contacted next of kin. He'd left all his worldly possessions, such as they were, to me.

I didn't have money or time for the journey, but I found both anyway. I wanted that ship. It wasn't fancy—just the same basic, reliable boat parents bought when their teenagers got their first interstellar license. He'd souped it up for long-range travel, but it was ugly as sin. All angles, no curves. He'd been ridiculously proud of it. He'd even painted it pea green. I hated that color. But it'd been his. I wanted it. I needed it, no matter how long it took me to get there.

My brother had never been one for sticking near home, so even a fast ticket would've taken weeks. If I'd completely cleared my savings, I might've afforded the fast ships. Instead, I booked a slow boat, hoping it'd give them more time to investigate. But they never found his body. I wasn't really surprised. He always traveled alone.

Idiot.

The Israu man running the storage hangar was typical—tall and hulking, with a knowing glint in his goat-pupiled eyes. Israu were always more intelligent than they had any right to be by looks. He sawed off the mooring lock with a grinder, then stepped back and cocked his head at me.

"Your ship?" He spoke in a typical Israu rumble.

"I suppose." I shrugged. "It belonged to my bisys."

He raised an eyebrow.

"My big brother," I clarified.

He nodded, watching me struggle with the sealing latch.

"We were surprised," he said. "Was in decent shape when it arrived. Considering it went into Rhem space. Mostly those ships come back as scrap. But this one? Just two major punctures. A couple of crushed struts. Very clean job. Not bad."

"You did the repairs, za?" I pressed my weight onto the latch and grunted. It didn't budge. "I was impressed when I got the holo-pictures, and I'm even more impressed now. I can hardly tell there was anything to repair in the first place."

"Wasn't much to do. Some blood on the walls, sure. But it cleaned up fine. My eldest girl finished most of it. She said this ship, eh." He lounged against the side of the ship. "It has some quirks."

"Dailyth rai—that's okay. It's been a while since I've flown this class of vessel, but I reckon I'll adjust." I jiggled the handle the other way, then tried leaning on it again. No luck. Heat rose to my face. Israu tended to view Draagoz as a weak but feisty race, and I

46

didn't like that I was probably reinforcing his biases. Nevermind he had a good ninety kilos on me.

"I didn't mean about flying. Never *flew* it. Girl doesn't have a license." He folded his arms and somehow became entirely neck and shoulders. "No, she told me. The ship has quirks. On the inside."

"Good to know. I'll keep an eye out."

"On the *inside*," he repeated.

"I don't think the ship will try to kill me. Thanks, though."

I pulled the handle towards my body a fraction of a centimeter. Something deep in the mechanism clicked enough for me to feel the jolt all the way up my forearm. I shoved downwards gratefully. The latch let with a hiss, and the door swung open. I flashed what I hoped was a grin. I couldn't remember if Israu smiled to be friendly or to be aggressive. I hadn't gone to the sort of school that taught that crap.

I was about to say goodbye when the image of my dwindling bank account flickered across the backs of my eyes. How much had the insurance company covered? I turned back towards him. "I don't suppose you refilled the fuel coils?"

He had—or rather, his eldest daughter had. So less than an hour later, I was on my way back home, pretending the sheer distance between me and the nearest terraformed planet didn't threaten to crush me with anxiety. Just point the nose in the right direction. Do the next thing on your list. Stay busy. Keep moving. Never stop.

The first quirk was almost a nonissue—sometimes the dashboard sensors would indicate the engine overheating. Every time I went down to check, nothing was detectable, either to my tools or to me. After a few days I wrote it off as over-sensitive instruments, but I decided to add an in-person check to every seven-hour shift—just in case—work, check, sleep, check, leisure, check. Dailyth rai, no big deal.

The second quirk was the door to the cockpit. It opened on its own sometimes, smooth as glass and silent as death. It freaked me out, and I hated it, so I jammed the door open, the emergency-shut trigger-ready—just in case. There wasn't anyone here to sneak up and surprise me while I was flying. Again, dailyth rai, no big deal. Once I made some cash again, I would fix both issues myself. In the meantime, I could live with oversensitive instruments and a faulty door sensor.

What was harder to live with, though, was the music.

He'd had a good voice. Resonant baritone. Pitch-accurate. Warm. He'd manifested Sound when he was about eleven. I remembered it because around the time most other boys sounded like squeaky hinges and nasal slide whistles, he sounded like the sort of announcer they hired for ad voiceovers. He started singing soon after, and he was good at it. He even got an Academy scholarship. If he was nervous at those auditions, he didn't show it, at least to me. My bisys smiled and ruffled my hair and informed me he was going to get the best scholarship he could. That way Mima and Bidyn wouldn't have to worry about finding tuition for both of us, and I could focus on school rather than money when I got there. He squared his shoulders and walked in, and he blew the audition judges away.

My brother left for Academy on that full-ride scholarship, and I followed the next year—different schools, though, and no scholarship to assist me. I had no particular talent or academic aptitude, and my Fire element was average at best. I'd hit puberty late, and my element system grew slowly. I was more interested in working with my hands than my head, so I found a technical school.

My school had practical classes, like welding and programming and business accounting. We learned to manipulate our elements for the good of our vocations. I got competent at keeping electronics cool, for instance. My element could absorb battery heat easily, and I'd snap it out my fingers in harmless little sparks. My personal devices never overheated. On the other hand, my brother's school had courses like Post-Worldship Elemental Watercolors and Draagoz-Israu Commerce in a Neo-Mersta Era. He was in choir every term. Mostly, I reckoned, his elemental education was posh but harmless. Maybe even useless.

My mistake.

I learned the extent of my misunderstanding once when we were both home on break. We were strolling through a station market during a layover while our parents refilled the fuel coils. I'd felt a sudden grip on my skinny shoulder and a tug strong enough to pull me off balance. I looked up to see a yellow grin on a stranger's face, smelled foul breath, and knew at the pit of my stomach what this stranger intended for diminutive, wiry me. And then my big brother was grabbing my other wrist, and the man had punched him across the jaw, and the boy I'd always known as bookish and artsy and gentle had turned with rage in his eyes, and he yelled so hard the tendons stood out on his neck.

A sonic wave rocked through my chest.

The man who'd tried to walk away with me fell to his knees on the steel grate, ears and nose bleeding. The nearest windows and lights exploded into shards, and the man collapsed forward, his eyes rolling back in his head. I'd never heard a body make a thud like that before.

My brother grabbed my hand, his face pale and certain, and we ran. We ran till we were out of the market, then hid behind a grimy food stall in a questionable housing district. We leaned over our knees and gulped for oxygen and tried not to throw up. I had questions—had he learned to do that at Academy, how come neither of us got hurt, would we get in trouble for breaking people's property, was the man dead, *what the fuck.*

But all my bisys said was, "Don't tell Mima."

So that was the third quirk: I heard his voice sometimes.

It seemed the walls were embedded with recordings of him speaking and singing. Despite the size of the ship, I never seemed to be in the right place at the right time to catch it clearly. But I could hear him through doors and down the corridor, muffled and unintelligible, but definitely *him.*

I had theories, of course: voice memos. Calendar items he was supposed to remember. Songs he was writing that he wanted to capture before the ideas disappeared. Custom system signals he'd recorded for himself. I knew someday his voice would probably stop popping up as the reasons he'd recorded it became obsolete, and I dreaded their disappearance. So I didn't try to seek the recordings out when I heard them on the other side of the ship. I didn't try to hear what he was saying, not clearly. I didn't try to figure it out. I could pretend this way. I could pretend he was just in the other room. I could pretend he wasn't dead. Stay busy. Keep moving. Never stop.

It wasn't a large ship, just enough for a cockpit, four sleep pods, a hygiene station, and meal prep, and then the cargo and engine bays beyond that. His sleep pod had been the first one on the left as you left the cockpit. I hadn't opened it yet. I couldn't bring myself to. But I took the sleep pod opposite, and sometimes when I was on my sleep-shift and I heard his muffled voice coming across the hall, I'd crack open my hatch and stare across at his. The hatch door was about three feet square, and like mine, only wide enough to slide through.

He'd chosen a terrible beige for the interior walls, almost as bad as the exterior puke green. And he must have known it was terrible because his entire sleep pod door was covered in travel stickers—places he'd been, presumably. I studied them in the blinking blue and green lights from the cockpit. Bri'Gran Academy. The Respite Cafe. Planet Mersta. Mo'Hachi station. Black Dog Saloon. He'd plastered them over the beige between the keypad and the crank-seal handle and again between the handle and the hinges.

I wondered what those places were like. I wondered what they meant to him. I wondered if he chose those stickers because he wanted to remember those places or because he wanted to decorate. I also wondered what the point of putting them on the *outside* of his pod was. He hadn't put stickers anywhere else in the ship—the beige reigned over all. So I laid strapped into my sleep pod, looked out the crack of my hatch door at his door, stared, wondered.

And I listened. Sometimes he seemed to be speaking, but mostly he sang, and through his door, I could half-catch snippets of unaccompanied solo baritone. It was his voice, unmistakably. Always his voice, just beyond the door. Sometimes it made me want to punch something, and sometimes I did. Sometimes it stung my eyes a bit, and I hid my face even though there wasn't anyone watching to make me embarrassed about crying. Sometimes I didn't feel much, so I'd lie there numb and paralyzed. Sometimes, blessedly, his voice was a lullaby, and I slept.

∽

"Wake up."

My eyes scrunched. The engine hadn't given any weird readings for about fifty hours. The ship had been quiet on the brother-recording front during my work shift, aside from maybe a murmur down near food storage, but that was about all. I was making good time, better than when I'd gone to pick the ship up; I'd reach my home station within five weeks at the rate I was traveling. The woman I worked for could only hold my job for six months, so the position would be gone by the time I got back. But it was worth it to have his ship. Things were looking, if not up, then at least level. I had turned on the autopilot and had slept peacefully.

"I said wake up." Warm, baritone, close, urgent.

My brother's voice.

This time my eyes snapped open.

My sleep pod was sealed and empty apart from myself and the belongings I'd brought in my duffel. My bisys wasn't here; of course he wasn't here. But I still held my breath and listened and peeled my eyes for movement, any movement. Nothing. Stillness. Silence. Darkness.

I released my breath slowly, letting my adrenaline-packed muscles relax. Well, then. A dream. Dailyth rai, that's alright, I'm okay. I'd dreamed his voice, but that wasn't surprising. I was in his space. I missed him, and I hadn't faced his room yet. I was tired and broke and honestly more anxious than I'd ever been before. Of course I'd heard his voice. Auditory hallucinations happened all the time. I closed my eyes again, relaxed against the straps holding me in place on my bunk.

"Wake *up*. You're in crossfire."

I swallowed as my eyes opened again and squinted at the empty room. He would never have made *that* sentence into a recording. I'd never heard his voice this clearly, this near me since I'd come aboard. Should I listen? Ignore it? I unbuckled the straps and lifted myself out of the bunk, then unsealed the hatch and bolted for the cockpit. Of course, I had to listen. Don't think. Keep moving. Never stop.

I had just barely strapped myself in and switched over from autopilot when the beam showed up on the scanning sensor. It was big. Very big. There were only so many ships that could produce a beam that size, but one of them was a Kyth war cruiser and the other a Rhem fighter. I wasn't going to take my chances with either.

I slammed the impulse engine to high and jammed both the throttle and the pitch as far forward as they would go. The steering didn't like the sudden change in trajectory and gave a loud, high, protesting whine. For a moment I was pressed backward against the seat, like the last few meters before the drop of a rollercoaster. Then everything reoriented, and I was off. It didn't matter where I headed, as long as I dove away perpendicular from these two behemoths. There wasn't hyperdrive on a ship this size, so my best chance was just to fly downwards in relation to them, as fast as I dared—and hope I made it out of the way.

"Kaaza taak!" I swore when something else appeared on the scanner. It rippled like a snake. "What is that? What the hell is that?"

The co-pilot computer switched on. It had an incongruously chipper voice. "Detected on sensor: Class F2 beam weapon. Origin: Kyth war cruiser."

"I know about that! The other one!"

Chirp, beep. "Detected on sensor: Class G5 energy grappling chain. Vessel unknown."

"What the fuck is a class G5 energy grappling chain?!" I demanded. I wasn't going fast enough to outrun it, whatever it was. The engine light flipped on—gaining heat too fast for the coolant system to keep up. The temperature was rising dangerously.

Pain and a shock shot across my chest, anxiety and adrenaline paralyzing my breath.

My breath. Now there was an idea.

"Divert half energy from life support to engine! Divert all energy from gravity drive to engine!"

For a few sickening seconds, nothing happened. Then a grate and a whine, and my ears popped. I could feel my chest pushing against the straps holding me to the chair, could feel my thighs lift off the seat. Good. Okay. The ship lurched, my shoulder blades pressed back in the chair, and we were going faster. Faster.

Above me, in the great expanse of space, two mighty weapons collided, exploding in reds and greens and blues, absolutely silent. Now I could see the ships they'd come from—huge, moon-sized, nasty-looking vessels which could, and almost did, squash my tiny ship without even noticing it was there. I stared up through the viewscreen as one beam after another shot out from the war cruiser. But no. I couldn't get distracted. I couldn't look up. I forced myself to look where I was going rather than at what I was running from, to point the nose in the right direction, to hold the ship steady. Keep moving. Never stop. Keep diving. Diving.

Diving.

About an hour later, I took refuge on an icy asteroid that couldn't have been more than a kilometer in diameter. From here, I could watch the titans battle. I could see them from above like a god, or from below like an ant. There had been three purple explosions, two red, one orange, five bright yellow, with a shower of sparks that fanned out like a disk. It would be pretty if it weren't so destructive. Like fireworks, without the smell of sulfur but with more dead bodies. I'd almost been one of those. They never would've known. Or cared.

I re-diverted the power again. The engine truly was overheating, with no false positives. I shut it down, shut down everything but life support and the blue emergency lights. I didn't bother to turn the gravity back on. As my neck and shoulder muscles finally unlocked their death-grip, I rolled my head back on my spine and released the pent-up breath I hadn't realized I'd been holding. I stared up at the ceiling. Terrible beige. Of fucking course.

The chest straps felt tight, so I unbuckled them. I floated out of the seat, turning myself around in the air, careful not to kick the dashboard controls. I pulled myself towards the engine bay.

There wasn't much I could do here, but I needed this bucket of a ship to get me home. I had to try. I opened the door. The heat hit like a wall. The elemental organ right behind my sternum pulsed, eager, anxious, a second nervous system that had just received the signal: *flee or fight*. Warmth crawled beneath my skin. Insistent. Hungry. Raw. The heat was too much, and I knew it. I didn't have the training, let alone the physique, to handle it. But if I left it, I'd be stranded. Stranded meant dead.

I'd be no better than him.

The engine hissed, angry and wounded. This was reckless. I swallowed and edged closer anyway. Move, I told myself. Keep moving. Inhale. Take the heat into your body. Ignore how your hearing goes muffled when your core temperature rises. Float to the airlock, pull yourself in, seal it. Let the heat explode off your body. Don't collapse. Swear a little. Stave off the pain. Move. Move quickly, before your element can absorb the heat again. Back into the engine room. Seal the door again, hit the release button before the walls start to melt, wince away from the violence of the heat rushing into space. Watch. Watching is moving. So watch to make sure the ice doesn't melt and become unstable. It doesn't. Dailyth rai—okay, then. You didn't die. Keep moving.

I turned back to the engine and started the cooling process again. Two times. Five times. Eight. Twelve. I tried to ignore how drunk and sick it made me feel. My chest hurt.

But after about an hour, the coolant system warning lights turned off. If I'd had a crew, we would've cheered. Instead, I hooked my arm around a railing and gasped for breath. Every time I moved, I left a trail of droplets in the air. Sweat. Hopefully the water-recycle system would collect it; I couldn't be bothered. My element ached against my ribs. The skin of my hands was dry and red. I might've torn a muscle in my abdomen. I took a deeper breath, gingerly, but nothing seemed to be broken. I flopped backward onto nothing and floated, staring up at the blue-lit ceiling.

He'd been there, hadn't he? By my bed. Waking me.

I swallowed, sealed the engine bay, and pulled myself wearily back towards the sleep pods. To the travel stickers on his door. My fingers traced the shapes I'd already started to memorize: ovals and triangles, letters and logos. Places he'd been. Places he'd loved. Places he wanted to remember.

The metal crank-handle was cold against my palm. I adjusted my grip a few times, hesitating. Maybe I wasn't ready after all. I was exhausted. I should sleep. I probably needed first aid.

Then I made up my mind and grasped the handle and turned it. The handle itself creaked, but the hinges were smooth and unresisting. I pulled.

My brother's sleep pod was tidier than I'd expected. Of course, at the moment anything that hadn't been strapped down was floating, but most everything important *had* been strapped down; at least that's how it looked in the dim blue glow from the emergency lights in the hallway. He had to have some recordings in here somewhere. Maybe I'd even find the music player that turned on most nights. Maybe I'd find a recording of him and listen. I pulled myself up and slid feet-first into the room.

The walls were plastered like his door, but not with travel stickers. With pictures sketched or printed or holo-screened. I reached for a light switch, but I'd turned that system off when I shut down the engine. Instead I floated close to the walls, close as I could without smacking my head. I touched one of the images. It was me, scowling at the viewer, my hair styled in an ill-advised and short-lived mullet. And another—our parents a few years before Bidyn died. They were laughing and looking at each other like they were a whole universe unto themselves. And another—a rocky outcropping towering over a group of friends in hiking gear. And another—our last family gathering following Mima's funeral. People. Places. Meals. The mundane, ordinary, and beautiful. I swallowed hard.

"Kaaza taak, bisys," I swore at him, but it came out small and quiet. I curled into a ball, and after a time I settled against his bunk.

The tears didn't come gently. They came like my lungs were being ripped out of my body. They came like Fire would explode from my veins. They floated off my face and hung in the air. They glistened in the emergency light, shimmering like crystal, but I couldn't find them beautiful.

I'd tried not to cry. I'd tried not to. He had decided to fly into unincorporated territories. He'd been an adult. He could make decisions like that. He'd loved the dark quiet of empty space, and I had never told him how much I hated him going out there because I knew my vehemence would hurt him. He gained inspiration out there where mortality loomed and eternity seemed like this moment. And who was I to tell him it scared me that he chased it? Who was I to tell him not to do it? He was an artist. He was a protector. He was my big brother. He was dead.

❧

I wasn't sure how long the sobbing lasted, but it left me exhausted. Somehow I'd floated up against the wall, my knees curled up into my torso, my elbows locked around my shins. Gradually I released the grip, and my limbs relaxed, floating, heavy, aching, weightless. My breath came slow and tired.

"Why?" I asked aloud, voice cracking. But I didn't know who I was asking, and I didn't expect an answer.

An answer came anyway, soft and warm and hazy and baritone.

"Sorry. I was too far in the black. They were fast. I couldn't outrun..."

I was too tired to shake my head, and I was afraid I might cry again, so I closed my eyes and asked the void, "What happened?"

"I remember—I think I remember—" His voice came again, spinning and muffled as though circling around my head.

Remember. Yeah, that was the painful part. I sighed and opened my eyes long enough to pull myself onto his bunk and strap myself in.

All his pictures. I made up my mind to study them more closely in the morning. I bet there were moments up on his walls that I would remember once I saw them. I bet the pictures would help. I'd look for a music player when I woke up, too. It'd be painful. Maybe I was ready, though. Maybe.

I hugged his blanket and squeezed my eyes shut. The cooling engines purred quietly several walls away. The life support system hummed and clicked. I took a deep breath. My bisys's voice floated around the sleeping pod, bouncing off the walls in soft ricochets.

"I screamed," he murmured. "I screamed at them."

"Who?" I whispered after the fourth time he'd said it. "The Rhem?"

A pause. Then, "They were a small crew. They boarded the ship. They hit me with a grappling chain and boarded the ship." He must've been scared. I didn't answer but gripped the blanket harder to my chest. His voice went unintelligible, overlapping mutterings, until, "I screamed until the Sound took over, and I just—disintegrated. I fell to pieces. Shaken apart by the sound waves. I remember, I think I remember, but—"

A dream. It was a dream this time, for sure. Definitely. Obviously. This time, it was my brain making things up. There's no such thing as ghosts. I knew that. My brain was telling me what I wanted to hear. It was using old memories and spinning them into hallucinations to make me feel better. People hallucinate in response to stress. I'd been stressed. This was a hallucination. I was a practical person. I went to a practical school. I had a practical job—when I could keep one. I wasn't scared—I was actually kind of grateful—but it definitely wasn't him. He couldn't be speaking to me. He couldn't. I kept my eyes closed.

"They say," I recalled from a years-ago science class, "theoretically, if a Draagoz person dies while using their element, the element might just swallow them up. The person might not actually die. They're just absorbed. So in a way, they're alive everywhere their element is used. And Bisys, maybe you're—maybe you're absorbed, too. But that's some sentimental bullshit. Right? It has to be. Made up by someone who refused to say goodbye. Someone like me. Sentimental bullshit."

Silence.

I took a breath. I *stopped.*

My mouth twisted at the darkness, and I admitted, "I want to believe it, though."

I was almost positive I could hear him laugh.

HOME TO SKJOLDEN

ERIK AMUNDSEN

I pour myself a glass of cognac and sink into my father's rosewood armchair. It's a long drive from Oslo. Nearly twenty hours on the road. My shoulders ache, my eyes hurt like hell, but worst of all, my head is empty. Just like the house. And very soon, the cognac.

It's weird without my mother here. She was always fussing about, making sure everything and everyone was taken care of. She should be relaxing in the Ekornes chair next to mine, sipping her coffee and asking questions. She'd get me talking about my work, then ask if I'm dating anyone. I'd say no, I'm not, and she'd nod like she's determined to stay out of my business. Then two seconds later, she'd suggest I move back north, and would be sure to slip in Simona's name as she shared gossip from neighboring farms.

The house is so quiet, I can hear the fjord water lap against the bedrock—a sound that's supposed to be relaxing. Maybe I'm just not trying hard enough. I kick my feet up, resting them on the leather footstool, and gaze at lithographs of tall, craggy mountains.

They've hung on these walls my entire life. I study the spruce bookshelves—one side crammed with works of Hamsun, Ibsen, Gaarder, and the other side packed with farming almanacs, and old newspapers from my great-grandfather's press. I glance over at my grandmother's quilt still draped over the back of the couch where my father took his afternoon naps. Everything's here—my parents' things are untouched. But the room is empty, like my head.

I'm restless. I get up and open the front window, and the air smells of salt and earth. At eleven o'clock at night, I have a clear view of the fjord thanks to the midnight sun. It never sinks below the horizon in June.

I stare out across the field to the mustard yellow house on the hill, and I can almost see the path Simona and I carved between our houses. There's a car in the driveway, but it could be anyone's. Maybe one of her sisters, home for a visit. I saw them a few months back when they came to my mother's funeral. Everyone but Simona, that is. That fucking hurt.

I'm back home a week early, wanting some time alone before my sisters show up with their husbands, their children, and their plans. Hilde and Anne are good at assigning tasks, to put it nicely, so the sorting and packing will be swift and efficient. It will be easier for them. My sisters already took the things they wanted on their many visits over the years. My mother encouraged me to do the same on my sporadic trips home, but I wasn't ready. The farm wasn't going anywhere. There'd be plenty of time.

My mom knew better. When I arrived earlier, I carried my duffel bag into my old bedroom and found a couple of boxes in the corner with my name in thick black ink. I haven't opened the boxes yet, but I know they're filled with things she knew I wanted. Things she wanted me to have.

My sisters and I are selling the farm. It was an easy decision. Hilde and Anne don't want Skjolden—they're already settled—but I think they still hope I'll want it. They know my parents wanted me to continue the legacy.

As a boy, I was excited to be the fourth generation to farm Skjolden. It's been in my family since my great-grandfather, Wilhelm, bought it in 1904, but the farm's much older than that. It's been around since the 1600s—the oldest farm in the parish—and it could've been mine.

That was the plan. When I went off to Uni, my life went in another direction, and somewhere along the way I forgot what I'd wanted. But my father never forgot. On my visits home, he constantly reminded me how much I loved Skjolden. Each time we brought in the hay together, or milked the cows, or went fishing in the fjord. And I would believe it again for a few days. When we worked together, I was capable. I was a farmer.

"You can keep it going, Johan," my dad used to say. "It's not a big farm, but you can make a living here." Or my father would bring up my legacy by reminding me of our family history. "I think a lot about your bestemor," he'd say each time he told me the story of how Grandmother Emma ended up owning the farm. By the time my great-grandfather Wilhelm died, her siblings had already moved to the city, got an education, and married well. My grandmother was the only one left. "As you know, they meant for Johannes to have Skjolden," my dad would say. "He was the oldest boy. But Johannes' couldn't run at the farm. Not after the way your great-aunt Sofie died."

My great-aunt Sofie was always the most interesting part of the story, because that was the part my parents never wanted to talk about. I only knew Aunt Sophie had died as a teenager after milking the cows in the barn one snowy morning when she was already ill with pneumonia.

When I was older, my father told me the full story. He said Johannes was haunted by his sister's death because he blamed himself. Sophie had told him she was too ill to milk the cows that morning, and when she asked him to help her, he said no. After she died, Johannes saw her ghost in the barn, and never again went out there alone—he refused. When Johannes became an adult, he left Skjolden behind for someone else to inherit.

I make a pot of coffee and fall back into the soft leather chair, my father's voice in my head.

"I know this land like my back pocket," he once told me. "And so do you, Johan." He pulled a ledger off the shelf. "Think we should we buy more calves? What about these milking machines?" he said, thumbing through a catalog.

I never had answers for him. I can't build things with my hands. I couldn't run a farm. I didn't inherit his abilities.

The summer before my father died, he was quieter than usual, but I could tell he wanted to say something. On the last night of my visit, he stopped in the doorway on his way to bed.

"When I talk about Wilhelm's legacy, I'm talking about taking chances. Something I didn't do enough of. You don't have to farm cattle. That was your bestemor's vision, not mine. Cultivate something new like Wilhelm did. Cultivate a community. That's what Skjolden was about, back in the day. I know what you're looking for, Johan, and you won't find it in the city."

It's high tide, and I force myself out of bed at seven in the morning. Half-asleep, I dig out a pair of my dad's old work pants, a tad big and a bit short, and an old button-down shirt. I head downstairs to the mudroom and pull on my boots. I have energy I haven't felt in a while.

I rush down to the boathouse, grab my rod, and head to the shore. It's been a while since I've fished, and I'm grinning wide as I cast my first line. The tension in my shoulders is gone. Within fifteen minutes, I pull a big saithe fish out of the fjord. Ten minutes later, I pull out a second and gut both fish on the smooth bedrock. The seagulls are screaming, flying around me like vultures. I throw the guts into the fjord, and they all dive, fighting for the prize.

I rinse the fish in the salty water, then walk back to the house and slice up the saithe. I toss the fish into a pot of boiling water with salt and vinegar, turn off the heat, letting them poach as I eat a few slices of bread and goat cheese for breakfast. When I'm done eating, I put the entire pot into the fridge and head to the barn, already looking forward to dinner: cold saithe with sour cream and cucumbers. I just need to find some potatoes.

I get to work in the barn, sweeping up, sorting through a million old boxes, hauling away trash. Feels good to stretch my muscles, so I keep working. As I'm going through my dad's tools to figure out what to sell, I stop and sit back on my heels. We can't sell Skjolden. It's been in the family for too long. Maybe I should give the farm a chance. Give myself a chance.

I lose track of time. I planned to work in the barn for a few hours, but I've been here most of the day. I stretch and survey my day's work, and my heart sinks. I've barely put a dent in this mess. My dad would have this place organized by now if he was here. Hell, even my sisters could have gotten more done. I have no idea what I'm doing. There's no way I can manage this farm.

When I get back to the house, it's half past four and I'm beat.

I'm covered in dust, cobwebs, and sweat, and I need a shower. But more than that, I need to eat, and I forgot to grab potatoes—something we've always grown at the farm. As a kid, I helped my father hill the potato field. It was hard work, but I liked that time together. It wasn't a big patch. Just right for my mother to grow enough potatoes, carrots, and rutabaga to last us the year.

We stored our root vegetables in the underground cellar. A big mound of earth with a small wooden door set into a brick frame. As a child, I hated going down here alone, and I made my trips as quick as possible. I would creep down the steps, shivering. Dreading the moment that the cold air would hit my face. It was my grandmother's fault. She was always cautioning me, saying I'd get lost down there if I wasn't careful. Those warnings sent chills down my back.

"Stop scaring the boy with those stories," my father would say to my grandmother Emma.

"But it's true," she'd reply. "A man disappeared. I saw it happen."

"Who did you see?" I'd ask.

But my father always waved her away before she could answer. He'd laugh it off, and the two of us would walk down into the earth together. We would sort through the crop, choosing seed potatoes for the following year. When we harvested a new crop of carrots, I'd help lug them down into the cellar, and I'd be in charge of covering them with moss to keep them fresh over the winter.

If I finished before my father, I'd organize the shelves of home-made preserves I helped my mother make after we went foraging together—the entire family went. We picked cloudberries and bilberries in August, and lingonberries in September, but cloud-berries were my favorite. After a long day, my stomach was fuller than my pail. Every summer I looked forward to foraging with my sisters and parents. Something I'd wanted to do with my own kids someday.

I walk out to the grassy mound of the potato cellar and open the cracked wooden door. The white paint is peeling, just like the house. I make my way down the steps, and that same old shiver runs down my back. The cellar is darker than I remember.

I reach into the closest bin and throw a handful of carrots into my bucket, moss and all, and grab a few turnips that still seem edible. The rutabaga bin is a further back, where there's less light, so I quickly grab one before moving on to the potato bins on the far wall. It's getting hard to see. But I know my way around.

With my pulse pounding in my temples, I rush into the darkness and fill up my bucket with almond potatoes. Turning for the door, my foot strikes something on the ground, and I go flying and hit the dirt floor with a loud *thump*. As I sit up to push the shovel out of my path, I hear a loud *crack*. The cellar door slams shut, leaving me in total blackness.

The darkness is disorienting. I stand and turn around several times, unsure which direction is out. With my arms in front of me, I creep forward until my hands hit a wall, then inch my way towards the door. My boot hits the bottom step, and I clamber half-way up, pushing against the cellar door. It doesn't budge. I climb up another step, crouch, and shove open the door with both hands.

Scrambling into the light, I fall on the grass, trying to catch my breath. My legs are trembling, and sweat runs down my face despite the cool evening air. My right leg hurts, but it's only a bit bruised—like my ego. I'm hungry, but I'm not going back down there. The fish will be plenty.

There's shouting down by the water. Teenagers, probably. No

need to spoil their fun. I walk around the side of the grassy mound to head back to the house and stop in my tracks. The vertical siding on the house looks newly painted, and the windows—they have those small glass panels I remember as a kid. Back before my parents changed them.

I jog up the steps and freeze in the kitchen doorway. My gaze darts around the room, taking in the wood stove, the oil lamps, the row of copper pots. In the corner, hangs cured leg of lamb, pork shoulder, and long strips of dried reindeer.

I spot a farmer's almanac on the kitchen table and walk over for a closer look. It's from 1906, and it looks brand new. The hairs on the back of my neck prickle.

Women's voices come from somewhere in the house, and I rush back outside before they see me. Dazed, I wander down to the fjord and find a crowd of people. Every inch of bedrock is covered with dried fish cover. Klippfisk—the salted dried fish my mom loved.

"Oh, here's someone I haven't seen before!" a man shouts, walking towards me. He's a tall man in his mid-thirties with a big beard. He's wearing a vest, thick pants, and boots. When I scan his features, my scalp tingles. I know those eyes.

"What can I do for you?" he says. There's an edge in his voice. He stops a few feet away and sizes me up.

"I heard laughter from the road," I say, relaxing my shoulders so I don't look shifty. "I'm looking for a place to rest tonight. A barn would be fine."

"I'm sure we can find you a proper bed," he says, adjusting his mariner's cap. "How about you give us a hand with the fish? It's not long 'til dinner." He shakes my hand. "I'm Wilhelm."

I smile at my great-grandfather, and my father's stories come to life. This is the entrepreneur I'd heard so much about growing up.

The man who farms new crops no one else in the parish ever tried. The first person to grow Norwegian Spruce for timber north of the arctic circle. The guy who starts a newspaper just to chew out politicians and government officials. He's a neighbor to everyone in need unless you cross him. I'm sure I can keep from doing that.

"I'm Johan," I say with a firm handshake.

Wilhelm raises his eyebrows.

"My oldest boy is Johannes," he says, studying my face closer. He points to a young woman on the bedrock. "Why don't you go help Ingeborg gather the fish."

"Ja, Herr Wilhelm," I say, nodding.

I make my way across the smooth bedrock, stopping when I reach the young woman. She's pretty. It's hard to gauge, but I'm guessing she's about twenty.

"Hallo," I say.

"Hallo." Ingeborg smiles.

She goes back to gathering fish, so I jump in and help.

"Those are interesting clothes you're wearing," she says. "Can't say I've seen anything like it."

I'm still wearing my dad's work pants, and the buttons on my shirt are open, exposing my t-shirt. I glance around. I don't stand out *that* much.

"It's the new fashion from America," I say. "I bought them in Osl—Kristiania."

Christ. I need to watch what I say.

"Wow, all the way from Kristiania. Do you live there?"

"About ten years now," I say. "How about you? Are you from around here?"

"I live on that farm over there." She points to the farm on the hill.

Everything clicks into place. Ingeborg was the kind grandmother who made brown goat cheese sandwiches for me and Simona every time I visited.

"What's it like living in the city?" Ingeborg sighs. "It must be exciting. All the theatres and automobiles. All those people."

"It's an interesting place," I say. "Folks are nice enough, but they're hard to get to know. They're not direct like us, here in Nordland. We don't have time for polite bullshit. I think that's what I miss most about this place. The people."

What the hell am I saying? I don't miss it that much. I don't think.

"Think you'll move back, then?" Ingeborg says it offhand, but her cheeks are pink. "Or maybe someone is waiting for you back in Kristiania?"

"Nei, there's no one waiting," I say. "I'd like to move back, but it's hard to find work around here."

I did it again. Am I just making small talk? I can't tell anymore.

"There are lots of opportunities in Narvik," she says. "The new railroad brings in tons of iron ore from Sweden, and they ship it all over the world. Mr. Johansen—Wilhelm—he lived in Narvik before he moved here. But he says there's too much pollution and politics there."

I know this story. My father loved telling the story of how Wilhelm made more than a few enemies in Narvik with his straightforward newspaper articles. And from what my father said, leaving wasn't Wilhelm's choice. The mayor and the police ran him out of town.

Ingeborg is staring at a man standing fifty feet away. He's a tall guy. Big. He's carrying stacks of fish and hauling heavy wooden boxes over to the outbuilding on the dock. He seems to work harder than anyone else.

"Is that big guy over there your sweetheart?" I ask.

"Petter?" She frowns. "He doesn't even know I exist. He likes Ragnhild over there, and she likes him, too."

I smile. I knew him as an old man. We called him Store-Petter because he was like a giant to us. And Ingeborg is wrong, he *is* interested in her. He was her husband. Knowing their future seems like a lot of responsibility. I worry I might screw it up somehow.

"I can't imagine Petter choosing her over you," I say.

Ingeborg's eyes grow wide. She thinks I'm flirting with her, but I'm not. I'm pretty sure.

"How old are you?" she says.

"Just turned thirty."

"You don't have a family?" she says, smiling.

"Nei, I've been busy working. I haven't found anyone to settle down with."

This is mostly true. I just haven't made it a priority. I've been on a handful of dates the last couple of years, but there's no one I've been interested in. Besides, after my father died, doing anything at all was a struggle.

"Are you back to see *your* sweetheart?" She gives me a nervous smile.

"I wish," I say. "She's probably married." A warm feeling floods my body. I miss her.

"Maybe she's not married. She might still be waiting for you. What's her name?"

"Simona," I say, frowning.

"Simona? I've never heard that name," she says. "It's different. I like it." She's quiet for a moment. "You heard there's a big barn party tonight? We're finally done with the fish, and Wilhelm makes the best heimbrent."

You can't have a party without moonshine. That's all there was back then.

"Dinner will be served in an hour!" a woman shouted.

It's my great-grandmother Hilda. I want to go say hello, but I don't want to piss off Wilhelm.

The women go inside, and the older men each find a comfy spot of grass for a quick nap after a long day. As I'm carrying the last barrel to the dock, someone kicks my foot. I trip and fall but keep the barrel upright. The guys all laugh, and a huge hand comes down on my shoulder. I glance up, and big Petter is staring me in the eye. It's not a pleasant look.

"Watch what you're doing!" Petter snarls. He picks up the barrel like it weighs nothing and carries it the rest of the way.

On the far wall of the hayloft, a fiddler and accordionist are playing polka. A few couples are dancing already, but most folks are standing in groups, chatting and taking swigs of potato heimbrent. They're all drinking straight from the bottle, and there are a lot of bottles.

Wilhelm's face is flushed. He's grinning and telling stories, making everyone laugh. He passes me a bottle, and I take a swig. It's powerful stuff—stronger and smoother than anything my dad ever made. Just one drink and my insides are warm.

"I hear you come from Kristiania," Wilhelm says. "It's been quite a while since I was there, and I hear a lot has changed. Were you there last year celebrating independence from Sweden? It must have been a big commotion when King Haakon came to take his oath."

"Ja," I say, thinking back to Mr. Hansen's history class. He was often drunk as a razorbill, but it made the lessons more interesting. And the days he was too drunk to teach, he'd have me run the class. After, I'd find his grade book and give everyone an A. The sad part is he never noticed. "There were thousands of people cheering when the king and queen came up Karl Johan Street in their chariot. I almost got lost in the crowd."

Wilhelm is talking about visiting Trondheim for the coronation, and I keep nodding, figuring it's safer to keep him talking.

"I bought Skjolden a couple of years ago." Wilhelm widens his stance. "I want to make this place prosperous for my children and future grandchildren. Hell, hopefully my great-grandchildren, too."

"It's quite a farm, I'm sure they'll appreciate it," I say. More families come walking up the ramp to the loft. The surrounding farms must be empty. "I bet you have big plans for Skjolden."

"Ja, ja. I'm going to develop the land. I want to grow some new crops—things no one else has tried."

"That's quite a risk," I say. "Why take the chance?"

Wilhelm takes another drink. "Because I can. I haven't farmed on this scale before, so I've been reading books and journals, learning as I go. Always learning," he says, tapping his head. "I want to be remembered as inventive and adventurous. A leader. I want to share my knowledge with my neighbors and develop this entire area. And one day my son Johannes will run this farm. He's a bright young man. He'll do well."

I think of my grandmother. If only Wilhelm knew.

"Skjolden will be in my family for generations. It will be my legacy."

I smile. "I'm sure it will."

The musicians start a song that fills the loft with whoops and hollers. Dancers pack the hay-strewn floor, twirling faster and faster in time with the music, and the floorboards bounce under my feet. Everyone is smiling, faces flushed from heat and alcohol. A pack of roving children play tag, darting and weaving between the flourish of skirts.

Swept up in the celebration, I take a few more swigs of heimbrent and ask Ingeborg to dance.

"I haven't danced the polka since my grandparents were alive!" I shout as we push our way into the crowd. "This might not go well!"

"No one forgets how to polka!" she shouts back.

"Don't be so sure," I say, taking her hand in mine. "Best keep your expectations low."

Ingeborg's smile turns to laughter each time I botch the steps.

"You *are* rusty!" she says, showing me the steps again. "Good thing you'll have loads of practice tonight." Ingeborg's more fun than I remember.

After a handful of songs, we take a break. I have sweat dripping down my face, but Ingeborg is beaming. She's radiant like Simona used to be, with those same bright eyes that make you feel special. Perhaps being stuck here with Ingeborg wouldn't be so bad. I shake that thought out of my mind and thank her for the dances.

"I'm going to cool off for a bit," I say, mopping my face with my shirt.

"Good luck," she says, pointing to a cluster of young women. "They're all waiting to dance with you." She puts her arms around my neck and hugs me.

"They'll be waiting a while," I say, hugging her back.

Petter is standing at the other end of the loft, scowling. Despite his warning on the dock, I go talk to him. I worry I've made things worse for him and Ingeborg.

"Hei," I say, trying to gauge his reach. "Why don't you go ask Ingeborg to dance?"

"Why? Is she not good enough for you?" He balls his hands into fists.

I take a small step back. "She's great, but she's not interested in me." There's confidence in my voice, even though I'm not so sure anymore.

Petter kicks a clump of hay. "She's not interested in me either. She's a farmer's daughter, and I have nothing to offer."

If that's the case, I'm screwed.

"I doubt she'd let that kind of thing stand in her way," I say. "At least not if she falls in love with you."

"I have a plan. Been working hard to buy a small plot of land," he says, relaxing his fists a bit, "but it's going to be years before I have enough money. She might not wait."

"Does she know this?"

"Of course not!" he says with a growl.

I throw up my hands. "Then tell her! You can't expect her to wait if she doesn't even know you have a plan. Take a chance!"

Petter narrows his eyes.

"Look," I say, rubbing my forehead. "My grandmother was a farmer's daughter, and she married a man who didn't have a penny—all because my grandfather wasn't afraid to take a chance."

His face turns red.

I hold up my palms in surrender. "Hey, I'm on your side!" I shout over the music. "I'm just saying you might not have money, but you carry a barrel of fish around like it's a teddy bear!"

"What's a teddy bear?"

"It's a toy that barely weighs a thing—you're strong. You're Store-Petter, for Christ's sake!"

"Store-Petter?" he says, trying the name on for size.

"Ja! I saw you out there working harder than anyone, and Ingeborg noticed you too. She told me she likes you, but you like Ragnhild."

"Ragnhild?" He wrinkles his brow.

"Sometimes you have to take risks. Now go ask Ingeborg to dance before someone else does. What's the worst that could happen?"

"I can't dance."

"You saw me out there—I'm a horrible dancer. You can't be much worse."

"Why are you helping me with Ingeborg?" He cocks his head.

"Because I messed up by not taking chances! I didn't think I wanted a farm until I met all of you, with your moonshine and your polka. I was so afraid of failing, I gave up without even trying. Just like I did with Simona! Don't you see?"

Petter takes a big step backward.

"I lost Simona because I couldn't get my shit together, and we drifted apart! I was stupid. And until now, my chances with her were slim, but if you don't go marry Ingeborg like you're supposed to, Simona won't be there when I get back!"

He stands frozen, his mouth hanging open.

"Oh god. I need to get back." I glance around one last time. "Tell Ingeborg and Wilhelm goodbye for me. I'm going to see Simona!"

I rush down the ramp, past a pack of sword-fighting boys. As I pass the house on my sprint to the potato cellar, a little girl hops off the front steps.

"Sorry!" I say, swerving. I almost knock her over. "Are you okay?"

"Ja, I'm looking for my brother." She's about five years old. "Do you know where he is?"

"I saw some boys under the ramp," I say, walking backward towards the cellar.

She follows me. "Where are you going? Somewhere fun?"

"I need to find my way home, and I'm in a hurry. You should go find your brother." I reach the cellar and swing open the door.

"You live in *there*?" she asks.

I pause at the top of the steps. "Kind of," I tell her. "I got lost in here earlier. I need to find my way back. But don't tell anyone I went in here, okay Emma?" I smile at her and shut the door behind me.

The darkness is absolute. My heart pounds as I inch my way across the cellar, retracing my steps to the potato bin.

"This has to work," I whisper. "It has to."

I'm shaking. I grab my bucket and inch back along the wall to the stairs.

This has to work. This has to work. This has to work.

At the top of the stairs, I take a deep breath and push open the cellar door. I scramble out into the night air, and the low sun shines right in my face—I can't see a thing. I let my bucket drop to my feet, and the potatoes spill out onto the grass.

My limbs are weak, but I sprint towards the house and drop to my knees when I see the peeling white paint.

Thank you, thank you, thank you.

I know I can get there quicker on foot, so before I can catch my breath, I'm back on my feet, running through the field. I follow the faded dirt path Simona and I made all those years ago. When I reach the creek, I take a gigantic leap and land hard. I stumble and scrape my hand on a rock, but I keep going. I haven't run this far in years, and my chest burns. Every gulp of cold air is painful.

I scramble up the hill to Simona's house, and my lungs hurt like hell. I come up over the ridge and see the car still in the driveway. It gives me a surge of energy, but a few meters from the door, doubt crushes me again. It's probably her sister's car. Or, if it *is* Simona, she's probably not alone.

I stop cold. What the hell am I doing?

I consider turning around, but the door swings open.

"Johan?" Simona says, stepping outside.

"You're here." My eyes well with tears.

I reach for her, and she throws her arms around my neck. Her body melting into mine.

"I'm here," she whispers.

I hold her like this for ages. A lifetime, perhaps. When our tears have dried, I take Simona's hand, and we follow the path home to Skjolden.

FLIGHT OF THE BUMBLEBEE

Susanna Skarland

The warnings were there for the world to see, signs of colony collapse flashing red years before the final hive fell. Although I barely knew my letters, I was old enough to read the struggle carved into my mama's brow. How she spent long hours laboring in the garden, tilling, seeding, picking. Long hours spent pollinating in place of the lost bees.

Mama had a family to feed—Grandma too stiff to bend her back to the soil, Grandpapa hobbled with his cane, and of course, me, the young one. I did what I could to help, but really, what could I do? She taught me to drag the hoses, to pick these plants not those, and to fetch the brushes sneaked out from Grandma's painting shed.

I used to lie in bed at night, listening to the soft whimpers of Mama crying alone in the dark. At day's end, after all her hard day's work had balled into determined fists, she would slowly unwrap those stiff fingers. The dark was a time to reckon with her conscious, to measure her successes and failures. There was no avoiding the dark.

Shortly after her 35th birthday, Mama buckled in the apple orchard, nothing but bones. She was my first dead body, but not the last. Grandpapa soon followed, and a few years on, Grandma succumbed too.

Today, bees' wings beat across my stretched canvas with each brushstroke. Painting is an indulgence, among the few remaining for me. The garden always needs tending, yet I cannot resist a palette in one hand and a brush in the other. A gift from Grandma.

My floppy straw hat rests on my head, tied loosely under my chin with a black satin ribbon I pulled from one of Mama's old dancing dresses. For inspiration. With the easel before me, I perch on Grandma's wooden stool, nicked and splotched with paint, in the shade of the stone shed's burnt umber door.

A slight morning breeze washes across my face. Cool, with a subtle hint of the scorching afternoon heat within the wind's grasping tendrils. Gavin is home early from the morning barter. He rushes in through the open gate and stops for a quick peck on my cheek. Sweat beads on his forehead, and I draw in a deep breath of his musky scent.

He leans in close, heat emanating off his sun-kissed skin. So familiar, so comforting. These paintings wouldn't exist without his support, his encouragement, his daring at the barter market. He knows how important the act of painting is to me. Not a moment to be wasted.

"What are they doing? Stinging it?" Gavin says, pointing at my rendition of honeybees encasing a dying wasp. A predator trapped by its own aggression.

"The clustered ones, maybe. These outer ones dance to signal the others. Looks erratic, but there's a pattern, a communication."

"Hmm," he says, his head cocked to one side. "I don't remember that."

"Honeybees used to surround invading wasps, beat their wings, raise the heat. A defensive move used only when threatened. Otherwise, they simply kept to themselves and foraged."

"Always working," he says, clicking his tongue. "Just like us." After a quick glance back at the gate, he kisses me once more. This time soft and slow on the back corner of my neck, meandering his delicious lips upward, nibbling my earlobe, and stealing my breath. "Will you be ready today?" he whispers, warm and airy.

I bend around and catch him on the lips. "I hope so," I say, rubbing my bulging belly. More than a flutter, a foot maybe, stretches in the confined space and pushes my taught skin against my palm. "I'm not sure how much longer we can wait."

"Then I'd better get busy."

Gavin latches the wooden gate and crosses the short distance to the house, around the neat dirt rows dotted with early starts of basic staples: tomatoes, spinach, carrots, and zucchini. Past the long line of rain barrels and over the series of hoses that snake out in multiple directions to the garden, orchard, house, and tub. Not a drop to be wasted.

Gavin scurries up a ladder onto the roof, and I drift back to my craft. I add the finishing touches of sun reflecting across a honeybee's diaphanous wings, translucent to the blur of purple lavender on the other side.

Standing up to gain perspective on the painting, I step back onto the shed's landing, smile. Tonal shifts from neutrals into deep browns and bright whites. Intricate details of light gracing the bee. My art improves with each painting, and this time, finally, the honeybee composition seems to pop off the canvas. Grandma would have been proud. The bees look as if they could fly.

Like Mama with her plants, Grandma taught me well, taught me her gift. She hummed as she painted, matching her tone to the width of her brush strokes. Loud and deep for broad blocks of color, soft and high for delicate details marked with a zero round. She infused her paintings with a breath of life.

So many years have gone by since I've seen a real bee, any kind of bee, let alone a honeybee. While wasps have thrived, the days of watching honeybees desperately flock the mint crowding the flowerbed... those days are over, confined to honey-sweet childhood memories. My garden and paintings are all I have left to share with Gavin. And soon, the new baby.

I lean into the shed, placing the new honeybee canvas inside to dry, and pick up another painting-in-progress. Like Grandma did before me with her own paintings, the shed houses my creations, canvas after canvas of color and movement and composition, of honeybees.

Outside, I pull the handle behind me. The arched wooden door creaks on forged-iron hinges whose flourishes meander along the door like wisteria searching for purchase. The latch and lever click, and I replace the padlock. I always keep the door locked. Always. This shed contains my soul.

Onto the empty wooden easel, I set the near-complete painting of a small bird hovering over a cup-shaped white flower. My mind's eye traces the outlines of both bird and blossom, unable to recall their names. I *want* to recall their names. Some things need repeating, or they will be lost to the past forever.

A sharp *knock* and commotion from the front yard return me

from my thoughts back into the garden. Gavin crosses the roofline to the front of the house.

"What's your business?" he calls, his voice carrying down on the breeze. And after a pause, he replies, "I'll be down in a sec."

The men do not wait.

The wood gate bangs open, and two men swagger into the yard—one young, in a gray uniform with a Pollinotics, Inc. security logo, gun in holster, and firmly pressed, too-perfect creases that run hip to ankle; the other man in a slick black suit with too much dinner hanging on his bones. He flashes his silver badge as if that means something, as if it gives him the power to do as he pleases. Above their hardened faces, the men's thirsty eyes soak in the view of the garden and the apple orchard beyond. After a moment, they fixate on Gavin, who is climbing down the ladder, and accost him. Of course.

"Gavin Rise?" says the one in uniform.

"That's me," Gavin says.

"I'm Vespa," the suit-man says, "and this is Dauber, from Pollinotics, Inc. We'd like to ask you a few questions."

"What do you want *this* time?" Gavin collapses the ladder and carries it over to the long side of the shed where he keeps the pick-axe and shovel. The men trail close behind.

"There was an incident in town today," the suit-man says. "A neighbor of yours was taken into custody. Illegal pollinator exchange. I don't suppose you'd know anything about it, do you?"

"I've been fixing my busted solar all morning," Gavin says, waving his hand upward toward the roof. "Trying to, at least. Don't know about any pollinator exchange."

"I see. The problem is," the suit-man says, loosening his tie, "your neighbor placed you in the market's alley. Right next to him, in fact." He lets the silence seep into a puddle between them. "You know what happens to those who flaunt the law?"

"Everyone knows," Gavin says. Of course, he knows. Billboards line the streets, ads flash on every screen, all reminding everyone, every day, in your face, how corporate robotic insect pollinators—Pollinotics, or Pollies for short—are the best, the busiest. What they don't tell you about is the brutality. And that the corporations mean to keep it that way. Anything for the money, the power. Food shortages? Hunger? No one cares unless you can pay. Those corp execs aren't the ones starving.

Gossip spread of this happening just last month. Enforcers bullied their way onto an elderly couple's property a mile down the road and trashed their garden while scanning for contraband. The enforcers planted evidence—an unlicensed Polli the couple could never have afforded, even at the barter market's prices. They were run off their land. No one knows what happened to that couple, or if they even survived. Yes, this suit-man has been lurking here before, traversing the neighborhood, preying on innocent people just trying to get by. I can sense it. His slow exacting movements, his keen eye. Steady, calm.

The suit-man clasps his hands behind his back and strolls out amongst the vegetables. He bends down low and caresses his fingers along the tender spinach leaves. Makes my stomach turn. His other hand taps against his leg, counting the number of plants per row, the number of rows, the number of trees in the orchard beyond. Just as the gossip said.

Calling the apple trees an orchard is generous at best. Eight trees total, they form a two-by-four grid at the back end of the property. Thick branches twist out horizontally from the many years of pruning to keep the harvest within a reasonable reach. In the autumn, their knotted trunks carry a heavy load. All planted and grafted by Mama.

At least five generations of my family had ties to apple farming, roots set down here as immigrants to the valley. Mama carried the touch like her mama and her mama before her. The touch went beyond the apples. Whether growing peas up crooked trellises in a small, raised bed or the present-day quarter-acre, Mama kept us fed, kept us alive. Now it's my turn to feed the family.

"Quite the garden you have here," the suit-man says. He tears a spinach leaf off the plant and stuffs it in his entitled mouth. "Must take a lot of Pollies to maintain." He arches an accusing eyebrow at Gavin.

"We make do with what we have," Gavin says, but the muscles in his jaw quiver.

"I'm sure you do." The man pulls out his screen from his pocket and scans through data. "Gavin Rise—one registered Pollinotic, first edition. Seems like one Polli that old would be working over-time to manage a piece of land this size. Now, you're sure you weren't up by the market this morning? Telling me now will save us all a lot of trouble." He pulls a crumpled cloth from his pocket, wipes his brow. Enforcer types are soft, aren't used to the searing midday sun. Not used to the heat.

"Like I said, I don't follow my neighbors." Gavin's voice wavers ever so slightly, like a faint ripple in a rain barrel.

The enforcers weren't even a *thing* until last year. Nobody thought that the corporations would ration robotic pollinators to increase prices and profits, and even worse how the politicians would enable them. Shows who's in whose pocket. And most people don't have that kind of sway. How else are the common folk to live, if not for scrambling, hustling up back-alley deals, bartering with neighbors and strangers alike? Otherwise, you'll find yourself forever indebted to the Polli corps.

After all these years of hardship, all these years of turmoil since the real pollinators died, since *Mama* died, I'm not about to pad these greedy bellies.

I hold out my arm and let slip my jar of rinse water. Glass shatters on the stone pavers like so many broken families before who lost their loved ones to rolling food shortages. Like Mama, like Grandma, like Grandpapa. Cold water splashes across my bare legs, an expected shock, but I suck in my breath, flinch. All eyes turn toward me.

Gavin rushes over, checks me for cuts, checks for glass shards. His expression asks if I'm okay, and I return with a simple nod. He knows. He continues to fuss, sweeping the glass into a jagged pile and washing the splattered colors from my swollen feet. He fetches another jar with clean water. All the while, the enforcers stand by, watching as if they have nothing better to do.

"We have nothing for you," I say, standing up and stepping back against the solid shed door. "Haven't you seen enough?"

"I wish I could say I had," the suit-man says. "But black market Polli exchange is a serious offense, and I would be derelict in my duties if I cut short my investigation. You know, those pesky rules and regulations. I'm sure you understand." His slow-burn grin paints a stinging smirk on his face, knowing full well it's the corps that need regulating. "And besides, this is the best part."

The two men exchange knowing glances.

The suit-man reaches into his breast pocket and pulls out a worn leather case the size of a fist. He slowly unzips it like he's cracking open the first pea pod of the season, with delicate and precise movements. The leather itself must have cost a Polli's worth of fortune.

I clench the shed's door handle. A faint vibration courses through the metal.

Unzipped, the open case reveals two pristine Pollies. But these are no ordinary Pollies—there are no clear plastic compartments for carrying loads of corporate pollen, no green fluorescent light flashing battery strength, no clacking wings. No, these Pollies are military grade, high tech. A sleek bronze for camouflage, an aerodynamic body designed for speed, and a distinct piezoelectric hum. These Pollies must have cost 100-fold the standard.

A few taps to his screen, and the Pollies twitch. Wings flicker. Another tap. The Pollies fly off toward the apple orchard. As they fly, their amped-up wings screech a piercing pitch, like the cry of a mother clutching her dying child.

In less than a second, the mechanical Pollies are lost to the eye save for the images they send back from their onboard cameras to his screen. The Pollies fly from blossom to blossom, tree to tree, systematically checking each newly sprouted flower for contraband robotics. Onboard nano processers return a data feed, but I only catch a glimpse of numbers and symbols flashing across the screen. With the suit-man's approval input, the Pollies proceed onto the next batch of blossoms.

The suit-man's final tap produces a beep, and the data stream stops. The Pollies return, landing back within their leather case and emitting a faint burnt scent as they cool off like an old-fashioned lightbulb filament. Ready to harass the next neighbor.

Yet the suit-man's attention lingers on his screen. Is this how it played out one month ago? My breath catches—heartbeat after heartbeat after heartbeat. Baby rolls and kicks in time as if trying to smack the screen straight from the man's grip. I already know what he's found—nothing. But that won't stop him if he dares.

The suit-man jabs his screen off and returns it to the confines of his jacket. And I relax my tightened breath.

"You're lucky this time," the suit-man says, thrusting a finger at Gavin. "Next time, maybe not so much."

I exchange a relieved glance with Gavin.

Hmmm!

A humming noise sounds from inside the shed door, and I grip the door handle. The enforcers spin around, ears cocked, eyes searching. Everyone stands, listening, staring at me. The sound from within grows loud, louder.

"Back away from the door," the suit-man says.

"But there's nothing in there. Only my painting supplies." I wave my hand toward the bird and flower painting resting on the easel. "That's all."

"I said, back away *now*."

"Please—"

Gavin rushes forward. The uniform-man steps in between us, his hand quick to his hip. He unlatches his weapon, and Gavin stops cold.

The suit-man swipes his screen. The Pollies glow a pulsating red and launch into flight. They quickly zero in on their target, coming fast and sharp, straight to the lock and latch. In no time, their mechanical appendages trip the mechanism, and the lock drops open like a punched jaw.

"No!" I say and swat at the Pollies with my straw hat. But no matter, they are persistent and dodge my swings. I try using my bulk to block the door. The paints, the paintings, the *honeybees*. I fumble, I grasp, trying to close the lock, trying to shield the shed from these dangerous invaders. The Pollies alternate ramming my hands. Sharp stabs that draw my blood.

The uniform-man wrenches my arm and shoves me aside. My elbow hits the stone wall, and a sting of lightning shoots down my forearm. Gavin rushes over despite the uniform-man's pointed gun.

"Keep them out of my way," the suit-man says and shoves my easel to the ground. My art lands face down in the grass, and my heart rises in my throat. The suit-man and his Pollies enter the windowless shed. These corps won't take from me, my home, my family. Not this time. Not ever.

I grab the pickaxe, wrapping my fingers tight. Two-fisted beads of sweat roll down my face, past my gritted teeth. The pickaxe above my shoulders, I'm ready to strike with crystalline resolve. But Gavin. He steps in front of me, places his hand on mine. His touch is tender, confident, melting my resistance.

"We'll be okay," he whispers. "You can paint more." He guides his callused hand across my belly.

I drop the pickaxe into the grass and slide into his waiting arms. And then the soft hums of passionate wings reach me as they reached me as a child.

I pluck my painting from the dry grass and set it on the righted easel. Greens and yellows and purples blur together in streaks across the damaged canvas. While the suit-man searches the shed, I dip my brush into my paints and hum the song of forests and foragers, of predators and prey. I hum the song of my family passed down from generation to generation, the song of our lives, both bitter and sweet. I sing for our unborn child. I sing for the bees.

The shed door slams shut.

Gavin joins my song, and the vibrations from the shed grow louder, rattling the latch and lever. *Knocking. Bumping.* A loud *crash*.

The uniform-man shoulders the door open and rushes in. The shed door slams shut behind him too. He bangs and bangs on the door, but the latch holds, and the door remains shut. A hum crosses the threshold all the same, a call and response with grunts and cries and gasps.

The resonant hum doesn't take long. Enforcer types are soft, unable to withstand the midday heat. And it's a damn hot day.

When the door slips open of its own accord, a rush of heat escapes into the early afternoon garden. All is quiet.

Beyond the keystone-capped doorway, filtered sunlight stretches over canvas after canvas. All blank, ready to absorb new paint.

In the center of the shed—two dead bodies.

Cast askance on the stone floor, lavender sprigs surround the two men who lie lifeless, drenched with sweat and unmoving. Their eyes pop from their faces, and their arms grasp toward the door like wisteria searching for purchase. Two dismembered Pollies lie in bits at their feet. All cut down like weeds in the garden.

"Okay, then," Gavin says, a tart smile spreading across his face. He stuffs the Polli pieces in his shirt pocket and the gun in his waistband. He gestures toward a blank canvas. "I'll get more paint tomorrow. But today? Are you ready?"

"More than ready," I say, fanning myself with a large paintbrush. "But what about them?"

"I'll dig the graves tonight," he says, "After dark." Of course.

Inside the shed, I right the blank canvases, straighten the jumbled tubes of paint, and sweep up the pile of sweet lavender. From the darkest corner, I gather paint brushes and small glass jars. As I exit the shed, I prop open the door with Grandma's old wooden stool. The time has come for some fresh air and a new crop of apples.

Gavin meets me outside with a short, steady ladder. He wraps his arm around my shoulders, and together we head out toward the orchard, to the apple blossoms. Painting with pollen isn't much different from paint. It is precious and exacting, time-consuming. And most of all, there's not a drop to waste.

We work our brushes from blossom to blossom, spreading pollen. It's not long before I hear the promise of the paint, hear my protectors spilling out from the shed. The hum and buzz reach me soon enough, surrounding both me and Gavin in a joyous noise. Gavin collapses into the grass, lowering me gently to join him, into a flurry of laughter and sighs.

I think of my mother and grandmother, how their craft moves around us in so many ways. If only they were still here to see their gifts bear fruit, to hear the soft, sweet pitch followed by the deep and lumbering resonance of diaphanous wings.

LIMINALITY

R. L. CASTLE

A girl walked in through the door.
Or, was it a woman?
No, it was a girl...

The latch bolt on the shop door clicked, and the line of tiny, round bells hung from the door's top rail sounded her arrival. Hardly bigger than a trinket, the bells were too small to ring and so rattled, instead. A single bell, its clasp tired and worn, fell to the floor with a tinny clink and rolled before the shoe of the girl that entered.

She stood 47 inches tall, halfway into the mid-panel of our six-panel door. Middle of the middle, we say. That would be tall for a six-year-old. At only ten myself, I didn't then know how tall a girl should be. But her face was round, and she held onto her mother's hand, so I knew the girl was younger than me.

"Don't touch that." The girl's mother pushed open the door

with a gloved hand and paused in the doorframe. She judged our shop, scanning side to side with thickly outlined eyes, heavy with mascara. She pursed her lips like she'd tasted something bitter. And while she acted like she'd never been in the shop before, I knew I'd seen her.

The girl, on the other hand, cast her gaze to the floor and kneeled to pluck the fallen bell and stick it in her pocket.

"Deirdre!" The woman pulled the girl up to a standing position and huffed. "Give that dirty thing to the shop boy and wipe your hands."

I set the can of peaches I was eating from on the counter and wiped my hands on the sides of my shop apron, so I could greet this customer with the handshake my father insisted upon. But my father appeared from the door behind the counter, wiping his hand with a clean rag that he stealthily handed to me. While nobody else in the back ever heard the rattle of the bells, they never failed to summon my father. For me, it was always the click of the latch bolt.

The woman strode to my father, the girl in tow, practically dragged along.

"Miller," my father said, hand extended. "How may I help you?"

She rolled her shoulders with an air of indignity and then whispered. "I need a new door."

My father pulled back his rebuffed hand and clasped it in his other. "This is a good place to start," he said.

The girl, completely indifferent to her mother's concerns, freed her hand from the woman's grasp, took the bell from her pocket, and presented it to me on her flattened palm.

❧

"Deidre?"

The girl takes a deep breath. "She's not here," she says and closes the door as she enters. It's a good, functional interior door. Six panels. Solid. Hung true. Its hinges swing easily for the girl, and her small hand latches it with a gentle, beautiful click.

I'm in my bedroom, I think. It's hard to remember. But these are my things. My slippers. My foot and prosthesis donning those slippers. My quilt stitched by my daughter. My book on the nightstand, its cover heavily worn like an archeological find. Next to that rests my father's old wallet, even more weathered than the book. The book and wallet sit in formation next to a pair of frameless glasses that I don't recognize but are probably mine.

I don't know the girl before me with a glass in one hand, the other outstretched with a pill cup perched on her palm. But, there are indications... Inside my wallet there's a photo, creased on one side and bent on a corner, of my mother as a schoolgirl that I've carried since she passed away. This girl's face bears a strong resemblance.

"Which pill is this?"

She shrugs. "I don't know what it's called."

"What's it for?"

"It's for your memory."

"It doesn't work," I say, gruff and intended for the universe, but the damage is all collateral. Her face falls.

Gently, I pluck the large oval pill from the cup. "Thank you," I say, "Um... um..." shaking my hand, prompting her.

"It's Daphne, Grandpa," she says.

"Daphne!" I reach for the glasses, and they fit comfortably across the bridge of my nose and have the perfect prescription. "It is you, Daphne. You know I can't see anything without these glasses. And you're so much less blurry with these on. Less blurry and so beautiful in your blue dress."

She tucks her chin and blushes.

She has my mother's face.

But she has Deirdre's smile.

The girl, Deirdre, let her head slowly tilt down, her cheeks mottled with rose and shame, her red dress adding a crimson glow. Not at the fallen bell, I was certain, but at her mother's public rebuke. The corners of her eyes wet with tears.

"Let me polish it for you," I said, picking the bell from her hand and wiping it off with the rag my father had passed to me. Deirdre watched me work at the crevasses while her mother and my father talked over our heads.

"The door was defective," the woman told my father. "It cracked when the wind caught it."

"Absolutely," my father said. "We pride ourselves on our construction. We'll make it right." He stepped behind the counter and retrieved a clipboard with various door sketches and prices. "As I recall, the last time we replaced your door, it had been damaged by the piano movers. Did they ever make that right by you?"

Deirdre stiffened and caught my eyes with her stare. With tiny motions, she shook her head.

The woman paused. "Yes. That's all resolved." She looked around. "Deirdre?" Even though her daughter and I stood only a few feet away. "Don't go far."

Deirdre took a deep breath and pressed her lips tight. She shrugged her shoulders at me. When I smiled at that, a smile appeared at one corner of her mouth. With my pocketknife, I cut the leather cord tethering a carpenter's pencil to the counter. The cord threaded easily through the bell, creating a necklace.

My father pressed on. "It hasn't been very windy lately, as far as I know. Are we sure it was the wind?"

Deirdre's mother squared her shoulders and spoke, again barely above a whisper. "I—I need a door that doesn't have a crack in it," the woman said. "Neighbors will talk. Can you help me?" She looked around and leaned in, a desperate lilt in her voice. "Discretely. Please." And as clearly as Deirdre had spoken to me with her eyes, so did the woman to my father.

"Yes," my father said. "Of course. One that can handle a good gust or two." Wrinkles of concern spread across my father's forehead, and muscles at his temples flexed. "My installers are fully booked tomorrow." When a moment of despair dropped on the woman's face, he added, "But I can come out early tomorrow morning." And when the woman's expression didn't change, he added, "Or tonight."

"Tonight, please," she said.

My father nodded. "We'll take care of you."

I finished the bell necklace by etching a D on its side with a sharp center punch and held it up. I knew that to others it was a tarnished toy. But I liked that rustic appeal. Keeping her eyes looking up at me, Deirdre tipped her body forward. I slipped the necklace over her head and neck. It stuck out, crude and out of place against her fancy dress. She clutched it and broke into a broad, full-mouthed smile, a fresh gap where there had been a front tooth.

"Let's not dawdle," the woman said and took up Deirdre's free hand. "They've got work to do." She towed Deirdre out of the store. At the front door, Deirdre looked back, still smiling, before the door shut.

❧

My granddaughter closes the door. I don't spend enough time with her. You need to see a person to know a person. Correspondence has its place, but it's not a substitute for being together. And you can't correspond with a child anyway.

I can recall all the times we read together or played blocks when she was still in diapers. But I can't see what I gave her for her last birthday when she turned... six. Or five.

Damn it.

My knees pop and back aches when I stand and settle onto my foot and prosthesis. I grab my wallet and book and head out into the hall. My aunt always complained, "I hate getting old." I don't hate getting old, just all the things that come with it. But complaining won't change anything.

Portraits hang in the hallway. Drawings by my favorite artist. Even my face is up there. But the hallway's different today. Perhaps they've been rearranged. Or maybe it's the lighting.

The crystalline voice of a woman talking on the phone drifts in softly from the study. Barely audible, there's a melody to the voice that I recognize. "Deirdre?"

She's busy. No matter. I need to make a stop at the bathroom, which is just a short walk down the hall. I'll limber up from walking around. Lying about all night makes my back and legs stiff.

The door to the bathroom isn't right. Somebody replaced it. One big shaker panel? It looks like a utility closet or a pantry door. It should match the bedrooms. I don't like this modern aesthetic.

"Who changed this door?" I call out.

"What door, Dad?" my daughter calls back from another room. She's beginning the day with attitude like she always does. And always has. I don't know why I provoke such aggression. I suppose it's because she's got too much of her mother in her. That makes me smile. Would I have it any other way?

I take a deep breath.

"The bathroom door," I yell back, though it almost winds me. "I'm not mad about it. But I could've done this right the first time if you'd just asked."

"Hey, Dad, I'm in the middle of something. Can you wait just a second?" Her tone has softened, but I don't need her to help me go to the bathroom.

The handle turns, but the door sticks. And that frustrates me. They didn't even measure this door to make sure it fit. In fact, the frame looks excessively narrow for this door.

I can almost hear my father's voice. *If you're going to do a job, do a job. If you're not going to do a job, don't do a job.* I'll fix it after breakfast. Plane the edges. Give it a new coat of paint.

I give the handle a good yank, and the door pops free. I stumble back with the door swing and against the wall behind me. My back and ribs smart, though the wall keeps me from falling. But the horror that descends upon me at the room through the doorway nearly drops me anyway.

"Deirdre!" I call out.

"Dad!" My daughter rushes into the hall, followed by my granddaughter. "Dad, are you okay?"

There are a thousand things I'm feeling, though I can't muster the words, and none of them are "okay." I can only point and shake my head.

My daughter offers to help stabilize me back on my feet. I wave her off dismissively, but she helps me, anyway.

"What do you need from the pantry?" she asks. "I can get it for you. Or Daphne will."

My granddaughter pulls a can of peaches off a well-stocked lower shelf and offers it to me.

∾

The store's door latch clicked, and I ran from the shop to the front, leaving my broom hooked at the shop door. There were two craftsmen working, but it was my job to ensure customers weren't left alone in the store while one of them or my father cleaned up.

The bells rattled as the girl walked into the store. Dressed in a red and blue ball cap and uniform, Deirdre looked as though she'd just come from a softball game. She let the door close behind her, held a finger to her silent lips, and crouched behind a rack of door hardware, hidden from view from the door, though clearly visible to me. She reemphasized her shush.

Her mother came in half a minute later, full of the air and attitude she always had—what my father called verve.

"Deirdre?" she called.

I glanced at Deirdre, hunched over, her hand still shushing me over her toothy grin.

Her mother followed my stare with her gaze and then looked up with an exasperated head shake, her curled hair bouncing off her cheeks. She approached the counter.

"Is your father available?" she asked.

"He'll be back shortly," I said.

"Oh?" she looked around and fluffed her curls. "He told me I could stop by anytime to inspect the custom doors I ordered."

"He needed a part for his Jack plane." He hadn't warned me that she would be by. "There's only one store that carries replacements, and that's across town."

She scrunched her mouth into a sour scowl and leaned over

the counter. "Well, do you know when he'll be back?" Behind her, Deirdre crept up, fingers curled up like the claws of a tiny dinosaur.

"Rawr!" Deirdre sunk her claws into her mother's coat, but the woman didn't flinch.

"Deirdre, act your age," her mother half-heartedly scolded. The woman turned to face the door and rested back on her elbows.

Deirdre scrunched her mouth into a scowl and came up beside her mother, leaning onto the counter with her fingertips and chin. Her scowl shifted back to a persistent smile I'd come to expect. "We won today."

"Good job!" I held out my hand for a high-five. When Deirdre went to slap my hand, she balked at the dirt and dust on my palm. Her hand hovered and danced, finally allowing only the pad on one finger to touch mine.

"I like doors," her mother said, surveying the front of the store.

This, I already knew. Most people only came to our store if they needed a new door. Even the most passionate door lover lost interest once they'd chosen. Not Dierdre's mother. I was sure that something besides doors drew her interest to our store.

"There are so many possibilities," she continued. "Each one says something different about what's beyond. Don't you think?"

I nodded. "I'd say it also says something about the person who picks the door." That's really the only thing a door ever says, even when matching an existing door. But you don't argue with customers.

Deirdre rocked her head side to side, eyes brightly locked on me, vying for my attention. Then she tapped her fingers on the counter. She had all of her mother's subtlety. Her finger pointed to the bell necklace I'd given her as a small girl. It looked too small for her neck and was nearly worn through.

But nothing would detract her mother's attention away from the front door. "My father used to say that when one door closes, another door opens."

"That's from Alexander Graham Bell."

She glared at me sidelong, like she sometimes did at Deirdre. "Well, great minds think alike."

That saying was right behind her, carved into a wood plaque above the door to the shop. But my father had cut off the second half of the plaque, the part that read, "But we so often look so long and so regretfully upon the closed door that we do not see the ones which open for us."

While Deirdre's mother talked, I pulled out some fresh leather cord and replaced the neck strap on Deirdre's bell necklace. I learned more about the woman's father, who claimed many others' sayings. I learned about beginning life poor and learning the value of savings and stability. And I learned that she'd left Deirdre's father only a year after he'd driven their car into their front door. He'd been drinking. I decided not to ask exactly how he accomplished that, as I'd gone with my father to replace that door, and they had two steps up to the threshold.

Finally, one of our craftsmen came out. He looked surprised to see a customer, though not surprised to see Deirdre's mother. "How can I help you?"

"I'm afraid I can't wait any longer," she said, checking her wristwatch. "Looks like I'll miss your father." She caught my eyes with a guilty look.

Without another word, our craftsman went back into the shop.

"I can show you the custom door," I said. "If you'd like."

"No." She paused. All of her typical confidence and verve abandoned. "I'll call and make an appointment. Deirdre? We're going."

"Thank you," Deirdre said. She clutched the bell necklace in one hand and pushed a folded piece of paper towards me with the other before she ran to her mother.

From the door, Mrs. Weaver called back to me. "How is your father doing?" Mortification crossed Deirdre's face as she looked up at her mother. But the question seemed sincere.

"He's doing okay."

"Good," she said, before walking out.

I picked up the piece of paper on the counter. It read, "Deirdre" in her fifth-grade scrawl, which was, to be honest, probably better than mine. Below it was a picture she'd drawn of the necklace and the bell.

I didn't recognize the picture for what it was.

My daughter is angry at me, now. But I told her, I don't want anyone's help getting to the bathroom. I don't *need* anyone's help getting to the bathroom.

"Oh really?" she said before storming off.

I hate "Oh really?" I've hated that since she was a teenager. That and how she would give me a one-word answer to a question and then shove food in her mouth so she couldn't answer any follow-up questions. I hope she doesn't teach her daughter to say, "Oh, really?" That would ruin such a precious girl.

Despite being angry with me, there is a piece of toast and a bowl of peaches waiting for me at the breakfast table, along with my granddaughter sitting opposite. But, despite that comfort, I'm angry because I counted eleven steps on the way up the stairs to the bathroom and fourteen on the way down. The only thing I'm certain of is that I miscounted yesterday, too.

Stairs have so many details with little to show for it. All stairs look alike in the end. If all that attention were spent on a door, it would be richly carved. Put your best stairs against a set of doors like The Gates of Paradise in Italy. Now those are doors. Stairs hold no significance compared to doors.

"Why aren't you eating your peaches, Grandpa? They're full of vitamins and fiber." She's so smart, like her grandmother.

"Do they teach that in kindergarten?"

"I'm in second grade," she tells me. "That's what it says on the can, 'Full of vitamins and fiber.'"

"Is your grandmother still on the phone?" I haven't seen Deirdre all morning. She must be very busy.

"Grandpa…" She puts her spoon down into her bowl of peaches, plants her elbows on the table, and rests her cheeks on her fists. A squished muffin full of frustration.

"I just thought maybe you knew, Deirdre," I say and then catch myself. Slip of the tongue.

"Grandpa…" Her eyelids flutter as though they sting. I've hurt her feelings, too.

I rub at my temples. Conversations can be so cumbersome at times.

"I didn't mean anything by it," I tell her, and it's enough because she goes back to eating her peaches. As do I, but the fruit is tasteless mush, and I spit it out.

My granddaughter stares at me across her spoon.

But I am ready with my defense. "Well, these are packed in water. There's no flavor to them. Where's the syrup?"

"You can't have the ones in syrup anymore. They're bad for you." She eats her bite, clacking the spoon against her molars as if to prove I'm being unnecessarily insolent.

"Who says syrup is bad for you?"

"My teacher." Another clacky bite.

"Second-grade teachers don't know about syrup."

"Oh, really?" she says.

I bring another bland bite to my lips but can't bring myself to eat it.

"If you're so smart, how many stairs are there?"

"Fourteen," she says.

"Are you sure there aren't eleven?"

My daughter walks up behind me with her bowl of fruit and toast. "There were eleven at the old house," she says and sits down to my right. "We had a raised landing."

My granddaughter looks to her mother and then to me.

"And this house has fourteen?" I say.

"Yep," my daughter says before shoving her mouth full of toast.

About a minute after Deirdre's mother left, my father entered the store, smiling—more than a trip to get a Jack plane fixed should warrant.

"You just missed Mrs. Weaver."

My father came to the counter, shaking his head. "I met Penelope as I pulled up. I think she'd been crying." He laid out a towel on the counter and rested the Jack plane on the towel. "Did you say something to make her cry?"

"I didn't do anything," I said, but the smirk growing on his face told me that he was teasing.

"Probably just a hard day. We've all had those." He reached out as if to tussle my hair but then withdrew. It's something that he'd done a thousand times before, though not for a while. It seemed off. Like the timing was wrong. I think he knew it too. "Come help me work on the Weaver door."

"The mahogany?" I asked.

With a nod, he headed back into the shop. I was right on his heels. I didn't get to work on mahogany. I was barely allowed to work with hemlock. I never got to plane. Normally, I got to sweep and empty trash and greet customers.

I put all the cut wood onto the bench—two long side stiles, three mullions, four rails, and six panel pieces that my father had shaped the day before. We set up the rails to be cut and routered for mortise and tenon, but at some point, my father took a step back and only directed me.

I was fine with that until he said, "We only have enough of this batch of mahogany for one door. So you best not mess up."

I stopped.

"I'm doing the whole thing?"

He shrugged and nodded.

"Not the whole thing. But it's time to learn a lot more."

It was at that point that I dropped a panel of the mahogany and dented one of the sharp corners.

"And this," he said, "is going to take a lot of coffee to settle my nerves." As he poured two cups, he looked back over his shoulder. "Deirdre told me to say, 'Hi.' I think that girl has taken a shine to you."

"She's a kid," I said.

"Good. Remember that." He came back with one cup that read, "The Boss," and another cup that read, "Not the Boss," and handed it to me.

"She's not the only one that's taken a shine to someone," I said.

My father shook his head.

"What does that mean?" I said.

"It means just that."

"She ordered a custom-made when our stock doors look almost identical. Don't you think that means something?"

"Could be," he said, which was more honest than I'd expected. "Could be a lot of things. Could be for comfort, knowing it was built just for her."

"It *could be* to watch you work and sweat and flex when you install it."

"Could be. Do you think your mother would approve?"

"I don't think she wanted you to be alone for the rest of your life."

"I'm not alone."

"I don't count."

"There are too many memories. Every time that door opens or shuts, I look up to see if she's coming to the shop to bring us supper. Every room in the house still has her presence." He hammered the rail into the stile. "And I don't want to lose that."

We didn't say anything more until we were finished for the night. With all the pieces assembled, we set clamps across the door to hold everything in place while the glue set overnight.

I held the shop door open for my father to go lock the front door. He stopped and handed me the key. I locked up, and as I handed back the key, I pointed to the plaque above the shop door. "Mrs. Weaver thought her father said that."

"A lot of fathers have taken credit for that one. Doors fascinate people. Why do the best jokes start with, 'A guy walks into a bar?' Why do you enter a room and forget why you were going there in the first place?" He held the shop door open for me.

I shrugged as I went through. "I don't know, why?"

He followed me through and shut the shop door. "I don't know either, I forgot."

That was so terrible and in the best way possible. I laughed.

❧

My daughter pours me a cup of coffee in a chipped mug that reads, "What day is it?" in faded letters. It will have to sit for a few minutes and cool down, but I love the aroma. I take in a deep sniff and let out a long, soothing, "Ahhh." I take a sip and burn my tongue.

"It's hot, Dad. Careful." My daughter has been busy on her computer all morning. Things irritate her when she's busy.

"Are you busy?" I say. "I mean, it looks like you're busy."

Her mouth drops open, and she looks at me bewildered. "I've been on calls with doctors all morning, Dad."

"I'm sorry, Menelopy." I reach out and take her hand. Her skin is so smooth and soft. Mine is spotted and thin. And her grip is strong. A lot of meat between her thumb and fingers. A hand that can wield a hammer or push a plane.

Her eyelids flutter. She dips her head and bites at her lip. "It's all right, Dad. It's not your fault."

"If you mean putting a bathroom door on the pantry, you're right. That's not my fault."

She pulls back her hand and takes a deep breath, shaking her head. She drinks her coffee from a mug that reads, "Proud daughter of a soldier" in a barely visible green. I'd be fine if the words on that mug just disappeared.

"It's just an old door, Dad. What does it matter where it came from?"

"Is that what you think about your food?"

"I thought you said, 'It doesn't matter where a door leads.'"

"What matters is what it means to you." I take a sip of coffee, and it burns my tongue.

"No, Dad, what matters is that I needed a replacement door, and we have a whole shed full of old doors." She makes a noise that sounds like a growl. Disturbing enough to draw my granddaughter back to the kitchen. My daughter trades glances with her daughter. "Look, I'm sorry, Dad. I just..." She stands up. "I just wish Mom were here." Her voice breaks, and she cups her hand over her mouth.

I push myself up to go to her.

"Stay there, Dad. It's okay." She wipes at her eyes and leans toward her daughter, tucking a lock of hair behind the girl's ear. "Stay with Grandpa for a minute, 'kay?" After an affirmative nod, my daughter leaves the room and walks outside onto the porch.

Deirdre walked into the store. At fourteen, she was still as tall as half the boys. It was a hot and sunny day, and she was dressed for it, with shorts that showed too much leg and a top that showed too much neck. And too much collar bone. And too much... other stuff.

But who was I to complain?

I, on the other hand, was covered in sawdust and wood chips, head-to-toe in shop dirt, and stained with sweat. I'd been planing doors all morning and had just stepped up front while my father ran out for replacement rolls of till paper. We frequently ran out of little things since my aunt had stopped watching the books.

"Hi," Deirdre said as she ran up to the counter.

I grabbed a rag, but it was pointless. Even after using it, my hands were still filthy. But she knew the drill and offered to shake. I held my hand out like a thing apart from me. She took it in a hearty shake that was too exaggerated and went on for too long. When she let go, her palm was covered in the same black and gray shop dust as mine.

On her wrist, she sported a leather braid with the tarnished bell, a D etched on it.

"Let me guess," I said, searching the counter for something cleaner to offer her. "Your mother would like to replace the pantry door next."

She smiled and nodded. "How'd you guess?"

"My father told me to say he could do them all at the same time."

She shook her head, her long flighty hair cascading in waves. "She says she wants time to think about them. She doesn't want to make a hasty decision."

"Custom?"

"Yes, but the same as the others."

"It's a pantry door. Don't you want it to look different?"

"I don't care. I don't think my mom does either. Just ask your dad to make the best kind." Then, with a softer tone, and quieter, she asked, "Will you install it with him?"

"Of course." He won't go over without me.

The bells clattered when my father came in through the front door.

"Deirdre," he said. "How's your mother?" He came to the counter with a bag of French fries and grilled sandwiches.

"Mom's fine." Deirdre took in a deep sniff. "Smells yummy."

"Would you like some?" My father offered the grease-stained bag.

She held up her dirt-covered hand, and my father immediately cast me a harsh glare. I scrunched my shoulders in a guilty shrug. He retrieved a smaller bag and took out a fresh napkin.

With cleaned fingers, she snatched a French fry. "Just one. Homecoming this year, you know?" Then she snatched another French fry and smiled coyly, presenting the savory treat to me inches away from my lips. "I just need someone to go with."

From behind her, my father shook his head.

Between Deirdre's forthrightness and my father's preemptive warning, I was left in limbo. I stood in the awkward silence I'd created and bit my lip like a fool.

My father shook his head again, one slow, precise, drawn-out shake.

I clenched my jaw until my teeth might explode.

Taking a deep breath, I took the fry with my dirty fingers.

Deirdre scanned my eyes and face as if she'd lost something.

"I'm sure that will be a sight to see," I said. "He'll certainly be a lucky guy."

Her eyes darted side to side, more frantically, desperate.

Her cheeks became mottled with red, but before fury could settle on her face, she pivoted on her heels and raced to the door. She didn't look back before the door slammed.

My daughter is back on a call. I'm eavesdropping. My granddaughter knows what I'm doing, and the wrinkles in her brow tell me that she does not approve. Scowling, she draws furiously on her tablet with her stylus. So I stick my tongue out at her. She sticks her tongue out in kind.

"I called this morning," my daughter says from the study. "Yes, Melanie Davis, that's me. I'm trying to find out if my father's tests are back." There is a long pause. "Uh-huh. It's for nanon therapy. I've been on hold several times already—this *is* the callback. Your clinic called me." Something slams down in the other room, and then my daughter stomps into the kitchen and roars out the mother of all f-bombs.

"Mom!" my granddaughter says.

"I didn't mean it, honey," my daughter says, hands on her hips, pacing quickly, turning tightly like she doesn't know whether to go back through the doorway into the study or march on through to the living room. "No, I *did* mean it." And she unleashes another massive ordinance. "Do you know what they said?"

"She meant fudsters," I whisper to my granddaughter.

"The results are in, but it has to be a doctor that gives the results, and she's backlogged." My daughter marches into the hall and comes back. "I need to get out for a bit. I'm going for a drive. Do you want anything?"

"Peaches in syrup," I say.

"Funny," she snaps. "I'm going to change, and then... I'll only be gone for an hour or so." Then she heads up the stairs. I listen. One, two, three... fourteen stomps total.

"Can you bring up the internet for me?" I point to my granddaughter's tablet.

She swipes across the device's face and passes it to me.

It takes a moment for the thing to notice where I'm trying to focus. "Nanons," I say when it locks on to where I'm trying to focus.

Nanon Therapy
- The use of synthetic nanites for cognitive enhancement and recall treatment in patients with Post-Pandemic Brain Syndrome. (see Contraindications)

"Contraincantations," I say. The tablet returns some schlock gibberish about horror movies and scantily clad witches. My granddaughter is not happy with my browsing habits.

I swipe that away and try a few more pronunciations. I know how to spell it, but I can't quite pull off this verbal monstrosity. It's a ridiculous word, anyway. I finger paint a circle around the word and show it to granddaughter. "Can you say that word?"

When she looks at the word, it breaks out neatly into syllables which she sounds out, and that gets me straight to the information I was hoping to find.

Nanon Therapy Contraindications:
- NSAIDs and other cognitive enhancers (may reduce the effectiveness)
- Patients with ACE2 and ZICI IV protein variants (affecting roughly 10% of the population of patients with PPBS-related deleterious effects)

My granddaughter slowly pulls the tablet I'm staring at from my hands.

"What does it say?"

"It says, I'm fudsted."

The day after Deirdre ran from the store, she was back. Her clothes were tighter, and she'd applied eye shadow and lipstick. She walked in with Don Cannon, a varsity football star, complete with letterman jacket and polished agate belt buckle. She practically skipped to the counter.

The store was extra busy as a cold spell had reminded people that they should fix and replace anything that didn't keep the heat in. Three of us were needed out front, including myself and my father. Don appeared lost at first but decided to post himself in the center of the store, forcing other customers to walk around him.

"Guess what?" Deirdre said.

As I was with a customer, I had to wait, though it wasn't long before the customer felt uncomfortable and said they'd be right back.

"Guess what?" she pressed.

I looked from her to Don and back. There are things you just don't say to customers.

"I don't know," I said. Possibly the biggest lie I'd said all year. Certainly, the worst, if not the only, I'd told Deirdre.

"Don's taking me to homecoming," she said. Like the day before, her eyes tried to scan mine, only this time it was a hostile attack. I looked right back. I suspect she was looking for a wince of some kind, any sign of pain. I guess I was looking for some sort of mercy.

Neither of us found what we were looking for.

"Just thought you should know," she said and spun like a soldier marching back to her escort. "All done," she told Don, who grabbed his belt by the buckle and gave it a hike. She left, glancing back for one second and then disappearing.

I felt my father's fingers on my shoulder. "Sorry, son. You did the right thing."

"Why's it the right thing?"

"She's too young."

"There are lots of guys from school that don't think so. They'd gladly—"

"And..." he said over me. "Because you're going to be in the Army for four years. It'll be cruel to let her wait for four years only to find out you've grown apart."

After everyone had gone, I was left to close the shop. I would fly out to basic in two months. I took out my wallet and pulled out a folded piece of paper. On it was Deirdre's drawing of a necklace and that stupid bell that had fallen off the door. And I saw how so obviously the necklace formed a heart.

I hauled back and kicked the door, solidly.

Again and again.

And again.

And again.

That damn thing was so solid nothing happened except for breaking my big toe.

⟿

I send my granddaughter to go watch her unicorn video when she informs me that she only watches Fuzzy Battle Monsters now.

Then I go back to my room. My granddaughter chaperones me until I close the door on her. The gentle click echoes in the mahogany. I consider kicking the door. My big toe on the sound side smarts to warn me that kicking doors has not always gone so well.

More durable than the original flesh and bone, the prosthesis might even better the door. A small consolation for the shrapnel that took it all in the first place.

Some things you recall with clarity. Making doors on foreign soil and then breaching them. And all the things that follow. It's a cruel irony, those things you can never forget and those things you struggle to remember. Or perhaps it's penance.

I can remember every word of every unanswered letter I wrote from the army hospital bed. But I can't remember my granddaughter's name. Or when I last saw my wife.

I pat the door as though giving it an apology. It's a fine door, one of the first I'd ever made. It's not this door that I see every time I close my eyes.

Not to be outdone by a toe, my residual leg is hurting. They ache in harmony. Like most evenings. I sit down on my bed. I reach into my wallet and pull out a yellowed piece of paper. It smells a tiny bit like sawdust. It has been folded and unfolded so many times that a hole has formed in the middle. Surrounding that hole, drawn by a young girl's hand, rests a makeshift necklace laid out like a heart. I press it gently to my lips and lie on my side.

A heavy thump from the hall stirs me, though I can't quite rouse from my sleep. Neither the whir of a drill or the rough handling of wood and brass brackets. It takes the definitive click of a newly hung door to waken me.

My room is dimly lit, but I know the thing in front of me.

It's a beautiful thing. A solid, toe-breaking thing, with flaking paint, weathered with imperfections, magnificent and more beautiful than The Gates of Paradise.

From the middle of the middle hangs a long cord with a small bell.

There's a knock, and a girl walks in through the door. Or, is it a woman? The silhouette framed in the doorway is slight but tall for a mature woman. My spirit flutters, reminiscent of the day she came through that door when I'd returned from a long voyage overseas.

"Dierdre?" I say.

"I'm here."

BETWEEN HELL AND FIRE

Bobbie Peyton

Fortunato and I are back in Elton, California for asparagus season. It's week five of a ten-week harvest on the Holdsworth farm. I saw more of America in the last year traveling the crop circuit than I ever saw of my home country, the Philippines, in my eighteen years. But rural towns like Elton all look the same. The farmworkers stay in the labor camps, and the town residents prefer it that way.

The crew of Filipino farmworkers, old and young men—manong and pinoy—rise before dawn. We stoop for nine hours a day with few breaks, bending at the waist and slicing asparagus out of the dirt, our brains baking in the sun—enough to drive anyone mad. The more experienced manong, like Macario, sway between the rows with an internal rhythm honed over decades. Fortunato and the other pinoys are slower but don't tire as quickly. Macario warned me my back wouldn't straighten for a while after that first day of stooping. He was right.

We must look the same, farmworkers out in the field wearing similar boots and long-sleeved cotton shirts, bandannas covering our faces. We all tie our pant legs, too. Fortunato once told me he did it to prevent anything from creeping up and biting his pecker. Being pinay, I have nothing to worry about there.

Dole Holdsworth, the owner's son, usually shows up in the afternoons to give the crew a ride back to the labor camp in his white Ford Ranchero. We call it the Shoe because it looks like a giant's slipper. That is the routine. Dole pulls up in the Shoe and leaves the engine idling while he surveys his father's land. Then he motions us with his Stetson. Those of us staying at the bunkhouse pile in the back.

But today is different. Another car approaches in the distance, where the edge of the farm meets the road and the land wavers from the heat. I recognize the sheriff when he pulls up to the farm. He has a scar that stretches from his right ear to his nose. Macario and I met him the last time we came through Elton. We were never formally introduced, but I remember the ridges of that scar, like the raised veins of train tracks winding through America's heartland.

Macario and I fled in the night, pursued by a mob of white men, with the sheriff leading the pack. Then there was the hollow cry of a train whistle and the clenching noise of the boxcar door meeting Macario's left hand. We escaped, leaving only two of his fingers behind. Maybe the sheriff has returned to claim the rest of Macario's hand.

Dole pulls up in the Shoe and chats with the sheriff before waving us out of the field.

"Boy, come here," Dole calls one of us over to them. Everyone knows he's talking to Macario, the *boy* who speaks the best English, even though Macario is much older.

I try to eavesdrop on their conversation, but the word "strike" is the only one I recognize. I understand English more than I let on and only panic when under pressure to speak it. The pruning knife's wooden handle is hot in my palm from my tight grip. I breathe easier when the sheriff returns to his car, looking pleased after their talk.

Dole invites me to ride in the cab. He and I are close in age, not yet seasoned and bent. He opens the passenger door of his truck like a gentleman and lets me ride up front with him, even with my clothes sticky with sweat. The rest of the crew has to sit in the back. We speed down the empty country road with the windows rolled down. Dole turns up the song playing on the radio and sings along with William Bell's *You Don't Miss Your Water (Till Your Well Runs Dry)*.

The truck stops at the bottom of the dirt driveway, and I linger behind. Everyone else scrambles out, rushing to be first in the showers.

"What do you do after work?" Dole asks.

"Walk," I say. I point to the trail behind the bunkhouse that leads to the Holdsworth's main house. It's better than staying cooped up with stinky, nostalgic men. The manongs usually spend their evenings playing cards and drinking beer, surrounded by a fog of cigar smoke. The pinoys make themselves up head-to-toe for a night on the town, while I wait for them to grant me the privacy to wash away the dirt from the field. They never invite me along.

"Do you ever go by the guest house?" Dole asks, clasping my hand.

"It's haunted," I say, remembering the eerie sounds I hear whenever I pass it.

He laughs. "It's where I sleep on hot summer nights. I promise you have nothing to fear. Meet me there tonight, and I'll prove it to you."

I pull my hand away and reach in my pocket for the knife. I never leave the bunkhouse without it anymore, especially after what happened to Macario last year. It is a knife for all seasons, and there is a comfort to feeling the weight of it in my grip.

Fortunato gave it to me as a gift when my ship arrived in Seattle. It was my first day in America, and he took me out for pancakes. Pancakes were the only American food I knew on the menu, and when we returned later for lunch, I ordered them again. Fortunato pushed a box across the table. He was wearing a silver ring he had bought for himself, wrapped with a band of abalone shells in different hues of blue. Inside the box was a hawkbill knife that folded into a blonde handle. Its two-and-a-half-inch blade curved out like a smile.

"My mother's afraid of ghosts," Dole tells me as he opens my door and walks me up the winding driveway to the bunkhouse. "She's suspicious of any new technology, too, and even refuses to install electric lighting in the guest house. She only allowed the main house to have electricity because my father insisted."

My mother once told me never to sleep in a room where someone had died. Their souls would haunt me forever. This man doesn't believe in ghosts and doesn't listen to his mother.

When we reach the door, I say goodbye, but Dole seizes my arm.

"Go tell Macario to come outside. I need to speak with him."

I pull away and find Macario in the bunkhouse. The smell of soap and brill cream overpowers the layered odors of dirt and sweat and cigarettes. Fortunato and the other pinoys fight over the cracked mirror and the nicest suit on the coat rack, where the men keep all their suits. Whoever grabs the best one first gets to wear it.

"Want to join us tonight?" Fortunato stops me before I head into the shower.

"I don't have a suit," I say, half-joking.

He pulls the smallest suit off the rack and tosses it to me. I shower, then try it on. It fits after I roll up the pant cuffs and shirt sleeves. I feel like a pinoy.

The air is charged when I rejoin them. Fortunato is reading aloud from a local newspaper about the strike.

"Front page story today, March 8, 1962. Hundreds of Tracy and Byron Filipino farmworkers walked out of the asparagus fields shortly after sunrise... The growers, their employers, have sent for the *braceros* to replace them, making scabs of their fellow farmworkers. The Filipino workers make less than a dollar a day and won't be paid for five more weeks, only after the harvest is done. They are at the mercy of the growers—between hell and fire."

Fortunato sets down the paper. "We should join the strike and support our brothers."

Macario lights up a cigar and rolls it in his mouth. "You arrive in this country young and tough, with all kinds of guts. But come see me when you've stooped in these fields for twenty years like I have."

"At least Holdsworth keeps a clean camp," another manong says. "I've seen some real shitholes."

Fortunato lets out a cry of disgust. "The drinking water smells like a toilet, and roaches are passing between the walls!"

"Holdsworth would kick us out of camp and withhold our pay if we went on strike," Macario says. "And it's dangerous business. I lost two fingers from the last—"

"Member dues paid in blood," Fortunato says. He then notices my ill-fitting clothes and laughs.

"Where do you think you're going?" Macario says.

"It's harmless fun, Uncle." I tell him about Fortunato's invitation.

"Those pinoys are wild. You don't belong with them. I worry about you."

He can't convince me to stay. What else is there to do? I don't want to run into Dole on my walk alone tonight. I ask Macario what he and Dole talked about outside.

"I won't be traveling with all of you after the season ends," he says. "Holdsworth has asked me to help prune the ferns."

I blink back tears. Macario has been more of a guardian to me than Fortunato, my own brother, and I may not see him again until next year. No one on the crew is allowed to stay year-round, and only the few invited to help prune the asparagus ferns get to stay on longer. The rest of us will either head north to Alaska for the cannery jobs or travel the California crop circuit. There are cherries in the spring, grapes in the summer, and lettuce during the cool season—the rhythm of our lives, measured by the new harvest and the changing weather.

"This has never been a good place for you," Macario says. "Where's your home?"

"Saoang," I say. "It's a small port town north of Manila."

His face falls when Fortunato comes to steal me away. "Don't lose track of time like you did before, Fortunato. You spent all night dancing and ended up back in the field with your suit on."

Maybe Macario leaving the crew is a sign that I should return to the Philippines. I didn't think my parents would let me come home after I ran away from the farm. But Fortunato wrote to them and they forgave me. Sometimes, I dream of starting each day leading my family's carabaos through the green foothills, with the blue ocean always in sight. Andadasi and mimosa plants litter the ground, signaling the time to return home by folding up their sensitive leaves at sunset. I have forgotten that feeling of home.

∽

"Where's Fortunato?" Dole Holdsworth asks Macario the next day.

Macario glances at me and shrugs. Most of the night is a blur. I remember eating dinner at the Chinese restaurant in downtown Elton. The waitress treated me like a man, serving me beers without batting an eye. Fortunato borrowed my pruning knife to cut his meat and never returned the blade. I had to borrow one of Macario's dull knives today to hack away at the asparagus.

We left the dance hall without Fortunato, assuming he got lucky with a redhead he danced with most of the night. I laid my drunk head on the bar and woke up when the lights came on. The dance floor looked dirtier and the girls less glamorous at closing time. Then I crawled into bed, still wearing the suit, catching a few more hours of sleep before another day in the field.

I begin to worry when Fortunato has yet to return the next morning.

"He must have wanted an American life," Macario says. He thinks that Fortunato has run off with the redhead. Maybe even married her. Her family will disown her for marrying a Filipino. No need to come back to Elton.

Stockton is nearby and has a Little Manila neighborhood, where they will likely end up. Fortunato will send for me after they settle in, I'm sure of it. He wouldn't leave me alone in this place.

After work, the manongs play cards and drink, and the pinoys go into town to search for Fortunato. They don't want me to come along without my brother to babysit me. I take a long walk after the air has cooled. The guest house sits between the main house and the bunkhouse, half an acre away. I hear the wails of restless spirits as I pass by. They seem louder than before.

I sprint toward the main house, hoping to outrun the ghosts. The sheriff's car is parked out front, and he's standing on the porch arguing with Dole. I duck down behind a bush.

"Whatever you need, Junior," the sheriff says. "But what did you do with the body?"

"It's underneath the guest house with the rest of them," Dole says.

The sheriff scrunches up his face with revulsion. "How can you sleep there?"

"Quicklime. Can't smell a thing. Or are you afraid of ghosts, too, like those flips in the field?"

"Will anyone come looking for him?"

"Doesn't matter if they do. He died in a farming accident. It's a dangerous business."

"Are strikes considered farming accidents?" The sheriff chuckles. "Doesn't have to be about the strike. He was breaking the law when we found him with that white woman—that whore."

My breath catches. Are they talking about Fortunato?

"I don't crack skulls over that kind of thing," Dole says. "They can't bring their own women over here."

"Don't they have a girl on their crew?"

"She's his sister."

They both laugh.

The sheriff leaves, and I steal back to the guest house. I look through the window, and my body shudders. A shaft of moonlight has lit up a part of the floor where there is a trapdoor. Its hatch blends in well with the rest of the wood seams, except for its steel ring pull handle. The trapdoor calls to me.

Nothing keeps me from entering the guest house. Not my fear or the sounds from hell, muffled moans that float up through the floorboards. Dole must not hear what I hear. If he did, he wouldn't sleep another night in this place.

I shake as I light the lamp. My heartbeat quickens, thudding in double time.

"You came," Dole says.

I jump a mile off the floor. He's standing in the doorway. I sit down on the bed, trying to calm my ragged breathing. The bed-springs creak as Dole lowers himself next to me. His chest moves with relaxed breaths. He places his hand on my thigh, and my hand steals to my empty pocket. I am no pinoy, even if I pretend to be sometimes. If I were, I wouldn't be so afraid of this man.

I catch sight of a glint of light on the bedside table. Dole sees me staring at the knife and picks it up to show me. He turns it in his hands, and the blade winks back at me.

"Beautiful, isn't it?" Dole gives me a knowing look. "Too nice for the guy I took it off—who probably stole it." He folds the blade back into the handle and places it in my open palm.

I know this knife—a knife for all seasons. I have cleaned and sharpened it every night since my brother gave it to me. It's the best gift I ever received. With it, I can stoop for nine hours under a blazing sun. I can take down Fortunato in a practice fight. With this knife, I am strong and unafraid.

I lift my eyes to Dole's face. It's soft and clean-shaven, like a young boy. A face with no worries. My body tenses, and I blink hard. I jump off the bed and move toward the trapdoor. I stoop down to open it and glance at Dole. His face changes.

I pry open the handle, and no voices escape. The moaning and wailing have stopped. I only hear the hinges squeaking now. The smell of damp earth rises up from below, and something else—rotten and dead.

"No!" Dole leaps off the bed.

I open the hatch wider. A small ladder plunges into the black abyss. Many hands grasp the rungs and climb—pale gray arms reaching toward the light and crawling up from the house's underbelly. On one ghastly hand, I recognize a silver ring decorated with blue abalone shells. I want to reach down and grab it, but if those hands touch me, I may descend and never return.

The dead are calling out again. This time, Dole's eyes widen with fear. He can hear them, too.

Dole rushes at me. He tries to grab me, but I shift my body, and he falls into the black mouth. I use his momentum and shove him downward, but he shrieks and clings to the hatch. The echoes of his screams blend in with the cries of the lost souls below, bouncing around the darkness.

Gray hands pull at Dole, but he holds on for dear life. I unfold the knife and slash the back of his hand. He lets go and fading limbs yank Dole's body down. His whimpers reach my ears, "Help me."

I slam the door shut and run.

There is only the sound of men snoring in the bunkhouse as I crawl into my bed and pull the blanket over my head. A rattle invades the quiet, and I gasp. It's the sound of a door banging against its latch.

I peek out from under my covers. The noise is coming from the front door—two men have entered without knocking. One of them is Dole's daddy, Mr. Holdsworth. The other is the sheriff. His hand rests on his holster, and his scarred face stares down at the men.

They speak with Macario, and then Macario turns to face me.

His concerned eyes hold on to mine as he calls me over. Sweat drips down the sides of my face.

"These men say someone saw you running from the guest house last night," Macario says. "Now, Dole is missing. Have you seen him?"

I shake my head. The other workers glance sideways at me.

"Come with us," the sheriff says.

"Where?" Macario asks.

"To the guest house. It'll help her remember what she was running from."

I gulp for air and look around for an escape, but there is none. I can't go back to that place. I still have five more weeks in Elton. Five more weeks of back-breaking labor, and the sounds of death that are driving me mad.

We march down the path to the door of the guest house. I hear a man's voice, wailing and sobbing. I wait for a reaction from the men, but they are unphased. Mr. Holdsworth is the first to enter. He looks around and then lets the rest of us in. Macario pulls me inside.

"Can't you hear him, Uncle? The scream of the damned?"

"Have you gone loko?" Macario says and gives me a hard shake.

The room is as I left it. The bed is rumpled, and the lamp has gone cold. But the trapdoor has disappeared.

I race around the room, searching the floor and following the single cry from below. The men look at each other in confusion. Macario stops me, and his three fingers grip my arm. I hold his hand up to his face.

"Dole and the sheriff killed Fortunato and dumped him under the house. So, I killed Dole!"

Macario shakes his head. "Fortunato ran off with a white wom—."

"There was a door in the floor. Now it's gone. But I still hear Dole's screams. They're all buried under this house. *Trapped.* The horrible things that happened here—on this farm—won't stay buried."

Macario's face drains of all blood. Mr. Holdsworth and the sheriff look back and forth between Macario and me.

"Boy, what's she saying about Dole?" Mr. Holdsworth says, only recognizing his son's name. I said everything else in Tagalog, and Mr. Holdsworth and the sheriff have understood nothing. But it is my story to tell, even if no one understands me.

"What happened to my son?" Mr. Holdsworth points a finger in my face.

"Leave her alone." Macario steps between us.

"Where is he?" Mr. Holdsworth's pleas match the ones coming from below the floorboards.

"What happened to Fortunato?" Macario shouts.

"You said you would take care of it," the sheriff says. "No strikes!"

"I convinced them not to strike."

"But it wasn't over, *boy!*"

My mind reels, remembering the night Fortunato disappeared. Macario had tried to prevent me from going out. Did he know something would happen to Fortunato?

The sheriff and Mr. Holdsworth keep Macario and me in the guest house for another hour. Their words fly out too fast for me to understand everything they're saying. Macario finally leaves, dragging me behind him all the way to the bunkhouse. To my surprise, he tells the crew that we won't work in the fields today.

We don't return the next day either. The men sleep in late. They practice fighting with their knives. The blades are not as long as the traditional arnis escrima knives, but they're good enough. We grow restless and bored. But we stay out of the fields.

Mr. Holdsworth comes to the bunkhouse on the third day. He and Macario talk outside. After Holdsworth leaves, Macario tells us we're going back to work—he negotiated a wage increase. Our routine is restored. Everything except the arrival of the Shoe to signal the end of the workday. And Fortunato.

The rest of the weeks drag by without incident. I don't sleep anymore, not since the night I killed Dole. Mr. Holdsworth finally pays us at the end of the harvest. Macario travels with us up north and doesn't stay on to prune the ferns.

We stop in Seattle before Alaska. The city is a balm to the isolation of the farm. There are so many young Filipinos arriving on the docks. Sometimes, I think I see Fortunato among them, with his swagger and shiny, dark hair. After all the months I traveled with the pinoys, from one farm to the next, I am still not one of them. But I have my own money, enough to buy a ticket for a ship headed back to the Philippines.

My eyelids sag as I stand on the deck. I grip the knife in my pocket. A radio warbles a familiar song, "You Don't Miss Your Water". I close my eyes and imagine the sun setting on the blue horizon. I taste the ocean air and see the andadasi and mimosa leaves folding closed. It is time to return home.

THE PANTRY GHOST

H. K. PORTER

Kate's feverish hallucinations swirled and disappeared. A man's voice had woken her, but it wasn't one she recognized. She opened her mouth to call out for help, but not even a croak came from her throat. Her chest tightened, lungs refusing to fill. Where was she? Maybe the voice was the doctor, talking to Cook. Kate knew she had been ill and was forced to go to bed. Had Father O'Brien come to hear her confession?

Mother of God. The delivery boy's letter! She had shoved it in her apron pocket, promising to deliver the letter to the master's daughter, Susanna. In the hustle of helping Cook with the big dinner party for the Fergusons, she had forgotten. Susanna had fallen ill that night, the first in the household to succumb to the Spanish flu. Scurrying up the stairs with a pail of cool water and clean cloths, Liam's letter was the last thing on Kate's mind. Dark spots on her cheeks, eyes sunken into blueish skin—Susanna gasped for every breath.

Just after dawn, Susanna died. Longing for a glimpse of daylight after her sickbed vigil, Kate glanced out the window and clapped a hand to her mouth. Liam stood in the yard, awaiting news of his sweetheart. The letter was still in Kate's pocket, and Susanna was dead.

Kate rushed for the door, but Cook grabbed her wrist.

"The house is already marked, girl! We're under quarantine now."

"But Liam! I forgot to give his note to Susanna! Please, let me return it to him—let me tell him. He needs to know I'm sorry." Weeping, she had collapsed at Cook's feet. "I forgot, and now she's dead."

Now, alone in the dark, unfamiliar room, Kate wanted to confess, to receive forgiveness, anything to make her feel better for failing Susanna and Liam. She tried to make a noise, a whisper, to let someone know she was awake, but still no sound emerged. The stranger's voice came closer.

"I found it at that huge brick building near the office. I thought the shop was shut down due to the pandemic quarantine, but the old man who owns it just hates people and refuses to post his business hours." Someone chuckled, and the voice continued. "The door was stashed behind a bunch of other salvaged doors. And look, it even fits perfectly in the frame."

There was a word etched across the glass pane. Tracing the backward letters, Kate recited them under her breath. Pantry. She recognized the script. It was the pantry door in the kitchen where she was employed as a maid.

The door swung open, and a cool breeze swept through Kate. She was face to face with two men. Two strangers in dungarees and undershirts. Must be laborers, she thought. No one respectable wore those kinds of clothes in public. Although Kate wasn't supposed to speak without being spoken to, she opened her mouth to scold them. They shouldn't be in the house. But her voice stubbornly refused to materialize.

"Now that the door's in place, the kitchen's finished. Kayla would have loved it." The younger man's tone was wistful.

The older man nodded and clapped him on the shoulder. "I know, Mack. Come on, time for a drink."

The door closed, and Kate was alone again. But wherever the men had gone, it wasn't far. She still heard their indistinct conversation. Ice clinking into glasses. No one was allowed to use the kitchen except Cook. Especially men Kate didn't recognize.

Kate recalled the last few days before she woke in the pantry. Susanna had died. The Fergusons' house was under quarantine, but it was too late for the rest of the household. Kate was the next to get sick. Guilt-stricken at failing her friends, she had begged for Father O'Brien to take her confession, but he never came. Kate's fever had worsened, and she had hallucinated her mother and her aunt, both of whom had died the previous year. Very few people survived the Spanish flu.

Jesus, Mary, and Joseph. Kate was dead.

She was a ghost.

Light filtered through a glass pane in the wood door. The pantry shelves were well-stocked with tins of peaches and green beans—familiar brands, but the labels were wrong. Kate puzzled over a box of gluten-free pasta. She'd never heard of gluten before, but Cook often used macaroni and spaghetti. And the little tins of cat food were fascinating—food, just for cats. Cook had fed their kitchen cats scraps of meat and the occasional raw egg.

A shadow fell across the glass pane, and Kate glanced up,

startled, ready to run if the door opened. But the men's voices faded away, and she heard the name Kayla again as an outer door closed. The rest of the conversation was lost.

Kate scrambled to her feet and tried the doorknob, but the knob refused to turn in her hand. She couldn't even make the door rattle in the frame. She threw herself against the door, kicking, and slamming her fists. But there was no movement, no noise, not even the sound of her breath, though Kate was sobbing.

Time passed. She didn't know how long she had been huddled on the floor, alternating between weeping and dozing. Kate heard the men's voices a couple more times as the light shining through the glass pane faded. Much later, she thought she heard a cat meow.

Sitting up, she wiped her face with her hands. A cat? Cook loved cats. They kept the mice from the dry goods and the moles from the vegetable garden. But the last cat had disappeared some months back.

A paw slipped through the gap under the door. Kate sniffled and reached out a finger to stroke the cat's white fur, but the paw disappeared. She sighed. The paw quickly returned, this time letting her run her finger along the silky-soft fur. Kate teared up again, grateful for the company, and made herself as comfortable as possible. Partially wedged under the bottom shelf, she kept her fingertips on the cat's leg, calmer now that she had contact with a living being.

The sun crept through the kitchen window, and as the interior of the pantry brightened, the cat left, and Kate got to her feet. Stretching her arms, she pressed her face against the glass panel, the novelty of the situation winning over caution. She could see the spacious room clearly, but it wasn't the kitchen she knew. The stove was sleek and black, not the white enameled range Cook took pride in. And next to the stove, an icebox, much taller than she had ever imagined. At least the sink was familiar, even if it was a shiny metal.

Footsteps sounded down the hall. Heart racing, Kate peeked through the glass again. Mack, the younger man from the previous night, was moving around the kitchen, running water, opening drawers, and peering in the icebox. The cat weaved around his feet as he dropped pre-sliced bread in a bright red appliance and pushed the lever down. Was it a toaster? Cook had told her about these newfangled electric toasters.

The cat meowed loudly. "Okay, Sheba. I know it's breakfast time."

Mack moved across the kitchen and pulled open the pantry door. Kate froze, unable to move or speak, but he reached past her, retrieving a small tin of cat food and a shiny bag from a shelf. Mack opened the tin, and Sheba leaped onto the counter. With an exasperated "tsk," he lifted the cat off the counter, set the tin on the floor next to a water dish, and opened the shiny bag. Kate caught a whiff of coffee as he measured coffee grounds into a machine and pushed a button.

Kate's mind raced. She must be stuck in this pantry for a reason, but she was no one special. She was just a housemaid. She cleaned the rooms and took pride in being efficient, unobtrusive, and a quick learner. Father O'Brien had told her time and again that pride was a sin, but it wasn't. It was who she was.

She rested her forehead against the glass, watching Mack eat his toast, and more questions rolled through her mind. He was dressed in dungarees and a white undershirt, but he seemed to be the owner of the house. Was that possible? Men never ventured into the kitchen to feed themselves. And if they had a problem with their cook, well, that fell under the mistress's responsibilities.

Sighing, Kate rubbed at the cold spot on her forehead, and Mack snapped his head around. His eyes met hers through the glass pane, and he paused. She held her hand to the glass, an acknowledgement that she was there and could see him too. He walked towards the door, a suspicious squint and scowl darkening his face. Kate waved, and he jumped back, startling the cat.

"Did you see that? Did you see *that*? "Mack turned to the cat, who was eating. "Okay, all right, okay, so, I thought I saw something moving behind the glass pane." His voice quavered as he spoke to the cat, who moved on to washing her face.

Kate pressed her nose against the glass. She wanted him to know she was there.

"Okay," he said, scrambling backward. "Is that a nose? I see a face!"

Kate grabbed the doorknob, wanting to try again.

"Oh, my God! Did you see that, Sheba?" Mack said, "The knob moved!"

Encouraged that Mack could see and hear her, she rattled the knob again. He stepped closer, hesitant, as if worried the door might burst open and a banshee would come shrieking out. Kate was light-hearted for the first time since she woke. When he came within arm's length of the door, she rattled the knob again. Mack recoiled slightly but reached out and opened the pantry door.

Kate blinked in the light of the kitchen. She hadn't meant for him to come so close, and she pressed herself into the corner. The cat rubbed up against her legs and flopped over, showing its white belly. She crouched and ran her fingers through its fur, once again. Kate was still worried he might yell or grab her arm, but the cat gave her courage.

Mack stepped into the pantry. He switched on the light, and there was a flare and a pop as the bulb fizzled and died.

"Damn it," he said, rushing off.

Kate heard him rummaging through a kitchen drawer. When he returned moments later with a flashlight, he pulled the door shut behind him with a gentle click, and a beam of light shone against the wall. The flashlight was much smaller than the one her da was so proud of, but it illuminated the entire space. He swept his hands across the shelves, inspected the door, the frame, and the glass pane, narrating his finds all the while to the thoroughly unimpressed cat.

"All right, Sheba, there's no one here except us. There's no access to the attic crawlspace or trapdoor to the basement. Oh, hell. It's nearly nine. Come on, I'm late." He herded the cat out of the pantry, double-checked the door was secure, and she was alone again. A heavy door somewhere else in the house opened and closed.

Kate leaned against the door and looked through the glass pane. A fluffy white tail flicked from under the table, and Kate "psppspped" to catch Sheba's attention. The cat sashayed over.

"Hello, Sheba. I don't know why I'm here." She gestured at the shelves even though the cat couldn't see her through the door and wouldn't care anyway. There was a strange comfort in how little cats cared about anything except naps, food, and the occasional cuddle. "Why can't I leave the pantry?" Kate sat on the floor, propped against a bag of rice. The cat snuffled around the door and again poked her paw through the gap, her purr loud even through the barrier.

"I remember when Aunt Annie died. Da and Uncle Samuel took the closet door off its hinges and brought it to the kitchen. They laid Aunt Annie on the door so Mother and the neighbor could prepare her body for her wake. For three days we all gathered around Aunt Annie, watching over her. Then Father O'Brien said mass in the yard, and Aunt Annie was buried." Kate put the pieces together. "I must have died right after Susanna. They must have laid me out on the pantry door."

Time slipped by, and the next thing she knew, Mack was home.

"Hey, Sheba," Mack said. "How was your day? Did you hang out with the ghost?"

Kate scrambled to her feet and looked through the glass. Sheba meowed, and Mack paused to scratch her chin before reaching for the pantry doorknob.

"Hey, ghost. I know you're in here." Mack stood just over the threshold, scanning the dim pantry. "Hell, I forgot to get light bulbs," he added under his breath. "I know you can manifest enough energy to move the doorknob, but can you make any other noises? Like knocking on the glass?"

She rapped on the glass pane three times.

He flinched at the sound. "All right. I guess you can. Um, I need a drink, and Sheba needs to be fed. Can you wait a few minutes? I really want to talk to you or, you know, communicate in some way. What about one rap for yes and two for no?"

She knocked once on the glass and he grinned.

"Well, all right then! Would you like me to leave the door open?" One knock.

"Great! Now, if you'll excuse me, let me grab Sheba's food here, and I'll be out of your way."

She watched as Mack fed the cat. A mundane act, but she had been so bored all day! When Mack left the kitchen, Kate took a few steps out of the confines of the pantry, and a movement caught her eye. Just outside the kitchen window, a faint outline of a woman stood gazing at the snowy white gardenia blossoms. Another ghost. Kate wanted a closer look, wanted to ask questions, so many questions, but Mack's heavy footsteps signaled his return. Kate was eager to interact with someone, anyone, but she darted back into the safety of her familiar little room. Besides, Mack was a man many years her senior, and her deference to men was deeply ingrained.

Mack dropped a handful of mint on the kitchen counter, their spicy, sweet fragrance filling the air. She savored the scents as he cut into a lemon, muddled a slice with a handful of mint leaves, poured whiskey, and added ice from a little chute on the left side of the black icebox. He took a long sip and sighed.

"Okay, ghost. Let's do this. I'm going to record us. I'm not sure you know what a cell phone is, but I'm hoping you know what a phone is. A telephone?"

She knocked once.

"Great! Okay! Well, a cell phone is wireless, and I can take pictures with it and video like moving pictures."

Kate knocked again. She had been to the cinema a few times before she had died, a special treat from her mother for her birthday and on holidays.

Mack pulled the small kitchen table across the floor and settled in a chair about six feet away from the pantry. He tapped on the cell phone and propped it against the whiskey bottle, his glass nearby. Sheba arranged herself on another chair and closed her eyes, uninterested in the humans but unwilling to relinquish her supervisory role.

"Let's start with some basic info." Mack paused, a shadow falling across his face. "Are you..." he cleared his throat. "Are you Kayla?"

Two knocks.

"Ah. Yeah, I hoped you were, but I didn't think so. Are you female?"

One knock.

"Okay, okay, good. Um, did you used to live in this house?"

Two knocks.

"Really? Then where did you come from?"

No knock, as she couldn't answer the question with either a yes or a no.

Mack sipped his drink, then realized his error. "Oh, right! Where could you have come from?" His gaze fell on the open door, and he slapped his thigh. "I'm a jackass! Of course! The pantry door! You came with the door?"

One knock.

"Huh. I mean, I've heard of haunted objects, like dolls and pictures, but never a haunted door. Do you know what year it was when you died?"

One knock.

"All right. Let me try decades first. The 1950s?"

Two knocks.

"Earlier?"

One knock.

After several more tries, Mack landed on the 1920s. Once he learned she hadn't died in childbirth, he asked, "Did you die from the Spanish flu?"

One knock.

"There's another pandemic going on right now, too, a century later." Mack summarized the coronavirus situation. Kate hung on his words, fascinated by the medical advances he referred to and appalled at the lack of progress in stopping the spread of the disease. Then Mack started discussing politics, and Kate grew bored. Old white men arguing about who could make her life better. Some things never change. She tapped on the door three or four times to get Mack's attention.

"Yeah, sorry, I'm rambling, aren't I? Okay. I still don't know who you are. Let me try something here. What if I recite the alphabet, and you knock on the right letters and spell out your name?"

A firm knock.

Mack smiled and began reciting, going slow enough that she had plenty of time to respond. Kate knocked when he got to K. The next time around, Kate knocked once at A, and then again at T.

"Is your name Kate?" Mack said.

An emphatic knock.

"Kate. Okay, Kate, is there, uh, is there another spirit in this house?"

Mack sounded diffident, but Kate sensed the desperate need for an answer. She thought she was the only ghost in the house itself, but she'd seen the ghost in the backyard. However, Kate had no way of communicating that to Mack if he didn't ask her the right questions.

Two knocks.

He deflated, disappointed and relieved.

"I was really hoping you were her. My wife, Kayla. She died three years ago from a brain aneurysm out there in her garden. One day she was just... gone." After a few moments, Mack took a deep breath and continued. "I found her when I got home from work. I have a landscaping service for the garden because I just can't be out there. When I saw you earlier, I hoped...Well, anyway, I'm happy to have you in my home, Kate. It gets awful quiet around here, even with Sheba around." Voice thick with emotion, he stood and refilled his drink.

This must be why she was here—to connect Mack with Kayla. She had failed in her mission to deliver Liam's declaration of love to Susanna. This was her chance at fixing that, of helping another pair of sweethearts. Kayla was the ghost in the garden! If she could somehow tell Mack about his wife or show him, maybe then Kate would be absolved of her failure.

The knocks, while useful, only worked to a point. Frustrated at her inability to tell him that his wife was outside, Kate stood up and shook out her dress. Mack jolted to his feet.

"Oh, God, I can see you now! You're not just a shadow anymore, I can clearly see your face! I can see you. Wow. Wow!"

Nervous, Kate brushed her hands over her skirt, smoothing out nonexistent wrinkles. She now knew her purpose—to reunite the lovers. Gathering her courage, she crossed the threshold and stood in the kitchen.

"Hello, Mack." Her voice was raspy after a century of silence.

"Kate. Hi, Kate. Oh my god—I can hear you. You can talk now?"

"Yes."

"You're sort of..." Mack waved a shaky hand. "There, but not there."

Kate looked down at her feet and hazily saw the floorboards through her boots. She drifted across the kitchen to the outer door. Kayla was on the far side of the garden, kneeling next to the lavender.

"May I go outside?"

"What? Like, physically? Yes, of course. Go ahead! You don't need to ask my permission." Mack splashed more whiskey into his glass before following Kate into the backyard.

The night was pleasantly cool, a crescent moon above the tree-tops, and a pair of owls in the distance trading calls. Kate was relieved to be outside and away from the confines of the pantry. She scanned the garden for Kayla and found her standing by the lavender, smiling warmly at Kate.

Kate lifted a hand in greeting, delighted that Kayla could see her now. Turning to see what Kate was waving at, Mack dropped his drink, shards of ice and glass spraying across the porch. Speechless, tears fell from his eyes. Mack's knees buckled, and he gripped the porch railing to steady himself as his wife approached.

"Kayla," he breathed. The woman smiled at her name falling from his mouth. "Oh, god. Kayla?"

"Sweetheart. I've missed you," she said.

Mack jumped down the stairs and sprinted across the yard to greet his wife. Kayla opened her arms, and he fell into her embrace.

It wasn't Kate's presence in the house which had caused Kayla to manifest. Kayla had been there for some years. Maybe in time and on his own, Mack would have stopped avoiding the garden, and Kayla would have appeared one night among her beloved plants.

Kate looked on, forgotten on the porch. She never had that kind of love in her short life, a love that persisted after death. Kate had grieved that she had failed to deliver Liam's letter to Susanna before she died. Now, watching Mack with Kayla, she hoped Kayla would be able to stay with Mack, at least for a while. As for herself, well, she had atoned for her failure and reunited the lovers. Was that good enough to move on, or was she doomed to haunt the pantry?

Sensing a presence next to her, Kate glanced around, expecting to see Sheba. Instead, she saw her mother. In a flowing dress, hair falling around her shoulders, Mary smiled at her daughter and reached out a hand to tuck a loose strand of hair behind Kate's ear. Kate smiled back, unsurprised at her mother's appearance.

"Did you do what you needed to do, my child? Right the wrong?"

"Yes, Ma, I did. Ma, why could Mack see me and not his wife who was out here for years?"

"He wasn't ready to see her, Katie. He thought he was, and he may have longed for her, but he felt guilty for not being here when his wife died. Tragedies happen. You and I know that better than anyone. When you appeared to Mack, he was able to open his mind to the possibility of seeing his wife once again."

Arms around one another's waist, Kate and her mother took a last look at the man and the woman in the garden.

"Time to go now, Katie, my darling."

Unnoticed by the lovers whispering under the night sky, a soft white light flared and dissipated as Kate and her mother faded away.

RABBIT'S KEY

STEVE GARRIOTT

The festival organizers had slapped a post-production Halloween sticker across a poster proclaiming, "A Samhain Celebration!" So much for cultural awareness.

"I don't have time for this," I said. If I didn't focus, my Analytical and Numerical Methods class was going to kick my ass.

"Can't you and your brainiacs, I don't know, whip up some reality where you aren't playing the part of a monk?" my roommate said. "All I know about theoretical physicists is they study all the time and believe in femions, which I can get behind."

"It's *fermions*." Proving once again we were orders of magnitude apart. But she did do all the cooking. I had to be practical.

"You can't be boring all your life, you know."

"Who says I'm boring?" I said. "Do *you* think I'm boring?"

"How can you not be boring with the schedule you follow? Don't you have adventure in your soul?"

"I can be adventurous," I said.

"Prove it."

No use backing out now or trying to explain the elementary principles of fermions to her. I couldn't resist a challenge! You don't inject yourself into a male-dominated profession without being tenacious.

I rummaged through her costume collection—third-year theater major—and pulled out a cape and related medieval accouterments: a forest green jerkin, a belt with a fake knife, and leggings. I'd have to wear my black and white tennis shoes because the curly-toed shoes were too big. One of her many boyfriends had been In *A Midsummer Night's Dream*. I spent a couple of dollars for some pointed rubber ears, and my transformation was complete—boring physicist to Salmy Ivyvale the wood elf.

Halfway through the evening, my hearing dulled by the band pounding out bad Stones covers, I nudged my roommate—dressed as a bobby-soxer—and pointed out a white rabbit. His costume was complete with an enormous pocket watch hanging from a chain. While the room was jammed with bodies, a sphere of empty space surrounded the rabbit.

"Adventures in Wonderland?" I asked.

My roommate gave a visible start, her eyes wide. "Oh, no, no, no!" Her hands went up, fending off my question.

"What, what, what?" I said.

"That's my brother, and he's a weirdo. He wears the same stupid costume every year. Why do you think no one's around him? We all know."

"All know what?"

"He's obsessed with some, I don't know... place. Thing. I could never get a straight answer out of him."

"What's the big problem? I'm not planning to, you know." I winked.

"Oh, great! I won't be able to get *that* thought out of my head!"

At this point, I couldn't help myself. I serpentined through all the festooned bodies, sidling up to the rabbit. "What's your story, Mr. Rabbit?"

The rabbit turned so fast, his head swiveled askew. He removed the head, revealing a young man, maybe a couple of years younger than me, with bristling eyebrows and a crooked smile. I could see the family resemblance in his eyes. They were intense, like his sister's.

"Uh, hi," he said. "If you really want to know..."

"I've been told I'm not adventurous." I tilted my head. "So, I'm being adventurous."

He checked his wristwatch; the fake pocket watch pointed at a quarter to twelve. "Cripes! It's almost time. I can't tell you too much because it'll wonk the experience. I need you to keep a clear mind. I need to find out if you can see something."

"Is that some kind of innuendo?"

He took a step back and stammered, "Oh! Hey, I'm not some kind of pervert."

"Uh-huh." I took a step toward him.

"Well, I'm not. Ask around. They know me. And anyway, we need to go now."

"Oh, I get it," I said.

"No, no, nothing like that either. Cripes! There's a place a few blocks from here. I promise it's legit. You said you wanted adventure."

I crooked a finger at my roommate. She tried to ignore me, and I stomped my foot. She owed me! She shrugged and surrendered.

"Oh, cripes, really!" he said, noticing his sister. "Is this some kind of Halloween joke? Am I on *Candid Camera*?"

"I'm her roommate, dummy," she said. "I'm vouching for you, so you don't have to show her your ID. I'll be a witness for the police report."

"Funny. You're a laugh riot," he said.

"How long will this take?" I said, interrupting the siblings before they wound themselves up. My voice caught him up short, and he pulled his eyes away from his sister.

"Not long," he said. "You'll know or you won't."

My roommate turned those intense eyes on me. "You don't have to do this. I meant you needed to get out, not end up on a hopeless scavenger hunt."

"He looks harmless."

"They always do."

"I'm standing right here, you know," he said.

"Yeah, yeah," we said.

The city grumbled with interstate traffic and the thumping staccato of a freight train. I jumped from the shriek of the metal gate. Witching hour jitters.

"Like I told you, no locks or *No Trespassing* signs," he said. "I've been here plenty of times."

I pulled my cloak tighter, losing myself in the hood's shadow. He'd pulled on a down parka over his motley three-piece suit, the prop gold watch outlined in the fabric like a huge push button. He carried the Mardi gras rabbit's head under his arm.

"Let the adventure begin!" he said, with a majestic wave of his arm.

Wonderful! I was part of a circus.

We stood in a simple courtyard formed by three old brick

buildings. The only light came from passing headlights panning across the walls. He looked giddy, like a kid waiting to open birthday presents. There was a bench, silhouettes of trees set in the cobblestones, drifts of fallen leaves. A window high on one wall was dark. He watched as I pulled back my hood, pulled off the pointed elf ears, and stuffed them into the pocket of my jerkin.

"These things have been itching all night," I said. "Where are we?"

"I don't know much about this place," he said. "I wandered in here one Halloween night and experienced something I couldn't explain. I've brought a lot of people here to see if they could see it, too, but nothing. One ex-girlfriend told me to get medical help."

"Did you?"

"Did I what?"

"Forget it," I said. "Okay, I'm here. Let's not stretch this out. What do I do?"

He put his rabbit's head on the bench and pulled out a small flashlight, playing the beam along the walls. "Call out anything you see."

"This is silly," I said, checking to make sure the path out was clear.

"Humor me."

I sighed. Play it through, I thought. "Fine. I spy with my little eye. Bench. Tree. I don't know what kind; I'm a physics major. Bricks. Door."

The flashlight slipped out of his hand and fell to the cobblestones. "Are you sure?" he said, the quiver of excitement in his voice. "About the door, I mean."

"Yes, I see the door. Looks like a plain wooden door. Nothing special."

He picked up the flashlight and lit up the door again. "Oh, my God! It's changed! I need to sit down." At the bench, he sat next to his rabbit's head. I stifled a laugh because he was serious. "Nobody else has seen that door before, other than me."

"Are you joking?" I said. This would be my adventure—a police lineup. Yes, officer, that's the door.

"It's not a joke. I stumbled in here about five years ago. I wasn't supposed to be out. I was wasted. Don't tell my sister. She'll tell Mom."

"Yeah, she's quite the tattletale."

He ignored me. "It appeared right in front of me. I didn't trust what I saw at the time. I had to come back to make sure. I've seen this door appear on that wall the last few Halloween nights. I see it, but everyone I bring with me sees nothing. But this time something has changed."

"What?"

"There's a doorknob." He stood, keeping the flashlight beam steady on the door. As he approached, the beam focused on an ornate copper doorknob in the shape of a dragon's head, its snout turned in profile. He reached out and grabbed the doorknob. "I've done everything I could think of to open this door. I thought about hidden latches. I felt for a key above the lintel. Nothing. Everyone was amused at my mime show. But now," his shoulders sagged, "it doesn't turn."

I walked over to his side. "I'm the first one to see the door and the knob? What makes you think I won't play a part in opening it?"

"You're right. It's so different, I don't know how to think. It's been hard listening to people call me crazy when I knew I wasn't."

"Here, then." I placed my hand on the knob, warm even through my glove. "Put your hand on mine."

The minute he touched me, the knob vibrated as if massive tumblers shifted into place somewhere behind the wall. I turned the knob, and we stepped back together as I pulled the door open. Through the doorway, it was night. The sky was a dark purple. The stars formed unfamiliar constellations. A path led around a bend. The flashlight beam highlighted trees with full foliage.

"What is this?" I said. "Like a conservatory in the building?"

"A conservatory with stars?"

"Technological stuff maybe."

"You're not the only one looking for an adventure. I've wanted to be a part of something like this all my life. To find my own rabbit hole." He took a step to cross the threshold but stopped. "It's like a pane of glass is blocking the way in."

"Hold my hand," I said, and then I put out a tentative foot. No resistance.

"You figured it out." He smiled. "It's open!"

"We can go in a little way to look." I couldn't stop shivering.

"Sure. A little reconnaissance. Come on, Alice."

"All right, Rabbit."

We stepped through the door together.

◠

CLASSIFICATION: TOP SECRET
[Organization name redacted] File#: 137-03599913
Profiles (Available upon request): [Redacted] AKA "Alice"; [Redacted] AKA "White Rabbit / Rabbit"
CONTENTS FOLLOW
West Coast AM transcript, KDWN, Las Vegas, NV; Dr. Cleveland Mornay (excerpt): Tuesday, 11 July 19--

"... Already doing some preliminary location scouting outside of Anchorage. These are touted as ionospheric investigations, experimenting with UHF and VHF communications. And while I agree more effective communications are admirable, the potential for using any developed technology for less than benevolent purposes is a temptation. If the U. S. military gets involved. Well, Art, we all know where this goes. Weaponization can't be too far behind. They are playing with forces, natural forces, which are the most powerful on this planet. If the power of, say, a tornado or a hurricane could be harnessed. Beneficial aspects, certainly, but we all know how easily the mind of man strays towards destruction..."

9-1-1 transcripts (excerpt): Thursday, 1 November 19--
Operator: "9-1-1, what's your emergency?"
Caller: "My daughter. My daughter is missing. I haven't heard from her since she left for a party on the 31st. She's not like this. She's responsible. I've never known her to disappear and not tell anyone where she is—"
Operator: "What's your daughter's name, ma'am?"
Caller: [Redacted]
Operator: "Does she live with you?"
Caller: "No, she has a dorm room at [address redacted]."
Operator: "Do you have any idea when she was last seen? Who she was with?"
Caller: "Yes. Her roommate [redacted] said she left the party a little after midnight with the roommate's brother, [redacted]."
Operator: "We'll send an officer around to check."

Telephone transcript (edited): Saturday, 3 November 19--
Rabbit: Alice?
Alice: Rabbit? Your sister didn't want me to call.
Rabbit: Thank God you're okay! You weren't with me when I came back. I thought I left you behind.
Alice: What *was* that? What happened?
Rabbit: I don't know. We weren't... us.
Alice: No. Somehow it wasn't me. I was in someone else's body. *Something's* body. How long were we there?
Rabbit: Maybe a week.
Alice: When you found me. I recognized you somehow, but it wasn't you, and I came back, it was only maybe two days. Time dilation. Or a drug trip.
Rabbit: A shared drug trip? No way. We experienced that. We were separated. I looked for you. Found you. For some weird reason, I knew it was you, too.
Alice: My mom was about to file a police report. Your sister is a wreck. She blamed herself. The door isn't there anymore. I need some time to process this, and my schoolwork! My classes! I'm a mess.
Rabbit: All right. Take your time.

Telephone transcript (answering machine tape; edited): Wednesday, 20 February 19--
Rabbit: Alice? You know who this is. Some weather we had there, huh? I about froze my ass off. We haven't talked for a while. I don't have anyone else to talk to about this. But I can't get it out of my mind. Do you realize how monumental this is? If it's true, we actually went to another place, time, dimension. Who

knows? Maybe even another planet. I read up on time dilation. Do you think we slowed down? Could be the reason why when we got back, not much time had passed. Like Ebenezer Scrooge, with everything happening in a single night! And I've been learning to fence. With all those swords around, I thought I'd need to know how to handle a blade. You have my number. Please call me back. Halloween will be here again before you know it.

Telephone transcript (edited): Tuesday, 26 February 19--
Rabbit: Don't hang up, Alice. Please.
Alice: This is starting to become harassment.
Rabbit: I know. I know. I'm sorry. I can't shake this. I've never experienced anything so profound. You're the only one. Nobody else.
Alice: You want to go back?
Rabbit: We came back, didn't we? It wasn't even us. We weren't actually there. For all we know, going through the door projected our minds but not our bodies. Astral projection.
Alice: More like a drug-induced hallucination. But it felt so real. Everything: the breeze and sun on my face. Cold water. And the air! So fresh.
Rabbit: It *was* real. More real than anything I've experienced. I could understand everything they said, or at least the ones I was related to. Living through his body.
Alice: What do you think happened to our bodies then? Were they being used by someone here while we were masquerading around in your fantasy land? Did you even catch where we were?

Rabbit: I didn't. But I didn't want anyone to know I didn't belong. That could have its own consequences. Alice. Once more. Please.

Alice: Time flows differently there. I did some calculations. We might be able to determine when we come back at least. Jesus! I'm talking like this was real! What if the person I was in is dead now? It didn't look like a very hospitable life. I can't go back blind. I need some answers.

Rabbit: You act like I'm somehow responsible for this.

Alice: I have plans for the future! What if our next trip lasts for years? I can't skip classes. And I have to think about my mom.

Rabbit: At least check with people. Let them know you may have to be gone for a few days.

Alice: You're not convincing me.

Rabbit: What can I do?

Alice: Let me think about it.

Record from [redacted] University library check-outs (edited; full list available on demand): 5 March 19-- to 1 October 19--

Patron: [Redacted] AKA "Alice"

Harriman, H. F., *Principles of Evolutionary Cosmology.*

Fazari, M., *A Discussion of Mathematical Constructs.*

Weinberg, S., *To Explain the World: The Discovery of Modern Science.*

Kaku, M., Collected Papers: *String Theory in a Field Form.*

Telephone transcript (edited): Wednesday, 15 October 19--
Rabbit: Alice? I didn't think you'd ever call.

Alice: Fine. We'll do this. But this is it. I can't jeopardize my career for this. I'm only justifying it because there might be a chance I can study the phenomenon while we're there. But how I'll study it without any equipment is beyond me.

Rabbit: Thanks, Alice. I'll see you on Halloween.

Alice: I'm sure I'll regret it.

Telephone transcript (edited): Saturday, 8 November 19--

Alice: What the hell, Rabbit!

Rabbit: What?

Alice: I was making progress! You pulled me back too soon!

Rabbit: You don't understand. It was a coincidence. I turned around and there you were. I grabbed you and BAM! We're back home.

Alice: I found their wise men, scientists. You'd probably think of them as wizards in this setting. Or astronomers. Geniuses! To think we have a corner on genius is absurd! Aliens built the pyramids? Bullshit! One of them, the *Magus* he called himself. He helped me see things, manipulating the components making up his world. I told him everything. About what happened to us. He said he knew.

Rabbit: He knew? How would he know? Like a prophecy?

Alice: Maybe. But something more organic. I could see he knew more but wouldn't say. When I told him about how we got there, he seemed to look through me. I have to go back!

Omaha Daily Courier: Friday, 7 August

DOZENS PRESUMED DEAD IN BLAST

(AP) – On Wednesday morning, units from the Adams County Fire District as well as surrounding counties responded to an explosion and fire at the Cody Agricultural Research Facility outside of Hastings. The loss of life is unknown. The compound surrounding the facility, which housed the families of the employees, was leveled by the blast.

Public Affairs representative, Loren Sievers, said the cause of the explosion was not currently known. However, materials regularly used in the research and production of agricultural treatments must be handled with extreme caution. The facility met or exceeded all government regulations. The blast was heard as far away as Kansas City and Des Moines. Damage estimates are in the millions.

Telephone transcript (edited): Wednesday, 2 December 19--
Rabbit: Alice? It's me. Pick up, please. Why have you been avoiding me? I know this was a bad one, but you've got to talk to me. No, I guess you don't have to talk to me. When, when you can, call me?

Telephone transcript (edited): Friday, 18 December 19--
Alice: They're all dead. Every one of them.
Rabbit: Alice? Is that you? You sound terrible. Who? Who died? Where?
Alice: In the... shit, what do we call it? The portal world. I'm done. That's it.
Rabbit: Wait. Hold on. I got there in time. I don't think we can die there.
Alice: I could feel the fire. My clothes on fire. My

skin crisping. No matter what I did, no matter what I said to those cretins. That poor woman. I killed her. But it isn't what bothered me the most. The whole redoubt, all those people—men, women, children—were slaughtered. All they wanted to do was help. To uplift. It was so real. Too real for this to be some kind of a fake, a construct.

Rabbit: I thought you were going to prove this was all a dream.

Alice: Don't be an asshole, Rabbit! I'm hanging up.

Rabbit: Okay, okay. I'm sorry. I didn't think you'd take this personally. Alice?

Alice: I'm here.

Rabbit: I mean it; I'm sorry. I guess I'm the one who sees it as a game. You're the one taking it seriously. For God's sake, I lost an arm last time! And it wasn't easy climbing a pyre with one arm. At least I was big enough to intimidate the locals.

Alice: I can't go back. I need to disappear for a while.

Rabbit: What do you mean by *disappear*, Alice?

Alice: It's better we don't talk about this, okay?

Rabbit: Fine. Whatever you say. But what about school? You can't just walk away. Alice? Alice?

RESOURCE REQUISITION Form 1-61803-3988

Requestor: [Redacted]

Organization: [Redacted]

Use of REAC-42 pinpoint gamma radiation projector approved. Limit use to subjects [redacted] and [redacted] per court order.

Status report, Friday, 1 April 19--

Despite concentrated effort over the last two (2) years, including the use of local private investigation firms (list of companies available upon request), government databases, and interviews, the location of [redacted] has not been determined. Surveillance of the ancillary subject, [redacted], and related acquaintances (list of subjects available upon request) has not provided additional avenues of inquiry.

Due to budgetary constraints, recommend reviewing this situation yearly. Resources should be limited to one (1) operative at ten percent (10%) utilization.

Another Halloween night, much closer to now.

Through the opening into the courtyard, I see a man in a winter coat sitting on the bench. My heart flips in my chest. He slumps, staring at the wall across from him. As always, there is no indication a door has ever been a part of this courtyard. His fingers wrap around the collar of the cane leaning against his right leg. He smokes a cigarette. He's shivering, though he's dressed warmly, with gloves and a navy-blue stocking cap.

Loose bricks in the walls twist out, the mortar gone. Unstable walls lean off true. Warning tape and signs notify passersby that the buildings are condemned and slated for destruction. I step across the fallen gate, but he doesn't turn. Traffic noises cover the sound of my footsteps.

I clear my throat, unsure if I will be able to say anything. "Hey, Rabbit. Those things'll kill you, you know."

The man smirks, takes another drag, coughs a couple of times. "Alice. Pretty much already have. But this one is medicinal. It's been a very long time. I wondered if I'd ever see you again."

"That makes two of us."

"The outfit looks familiar."

I raise my arms, and the cape billows out. "This old thing? It all still fits, too. Worked my ass off. But I couldn't find the ears."

"Check your pocket."

I pull the two rubber ears from my jerkin pocket and laugh. "You remembered."

"Hard to forget that first night. I wondered if you'd come."

"I wondered if I would too," I said. "Let's say I've been trying to keep a low profile."

"The lowest."

"I talked to your sister. Clandestinely, of course. I've learned a few tricks over the years." I pull a cell phone out of my pocket and toss it into one of the metal debris-filled trash cans. The device combusts—a flash, a sizzle, smoke, and the smell of hot wires and rubber insulation. One of my party tricks. "Your sister said you'd left the house about an hour ago and was worried about you. I was worried, too, but I had an idea where I'd find you. Halloween night? No brainer. Unfortunately, I'm probably not the only one who could figure it out. We should be okay tonight, though."

He looks up at me. His eyes are hollow, his skin jaundiced. "What do you mean?"

"Never mind. You didn't walk the whole way, did you?"

"I Ubered over. I know my limits. You and my sister still pretty chummy?"

"Every year we talk," I say. "Just to check up on you."

He coughs again. "Next time you talk to her, tell her she needs to get a life."

"It's her choice. God knows you need someone to look after you. You should feel lucky she can deal with you. She knows you're an asshole but with a heart of gold."

"Interesting metaphor." He stands, leaning heavily on the cane. "I tried this with lots of other people, you know. Nothing happened."

"I guess the two of us are the only ones who can step through the looking glass."

"True." He nods. "The end of a dynasty. What, twenty years or something?"

"Thirty-two," I say.

He chuckles. "You always have the data, huh, Scully?"

"Yep."

"Did Sis tell you anything?" he says.

"She said you were ending treatment."

"I'm no doctor, but I'm not stupid."

"Never said you were."

"I came down here after the earthquake. I had a bad feeling about the buildings. Their age. Most of them weren't retrofitted. I know a couple crumbled. Flies in the face of 'they don't make them like they used to.'"

"But our wall stood the test," I say.

"For now."

"For now."

"I didn't want to ask you to come. I thought maybe it would work one time for me. I've been able to see the door, but without you, there's no way to open it."

"And I swoop in and save the day."

He smiles and removes the stocking cap. He's bald from the chemo. "This thing itches like you wouldn't believe."

"I know. Like my rubber ears." I drop the hood; my head is shaved too.

"Cripes, that's unexpected!"

"Ah, come on. It fits with the whole story. The knight enters and saves the damsel in distress."

"Now I'm a damsel," he says.

"I'm sure it's symbolic of something. Friendship, maybe? I'm trying to come up with a pun about follicles, but I got nothin.'"

"Look who's getting symbolic all of the sudden," he says.

"Didn't mean to steal your thunder."

"You didn't have to do that."

"I kinda did. Wanted to show you I've always cared. That's never changed. We go back a long way. Been through some amazing, shocking, beautiful lives. How many people can say they've lived more than one life?"

"Padded the pockets of a bunch of therapists."

"That too," I say.

"This will probably be the last time. Pretty sure the demolition for these buildings is going to be in the next few weeks. The city told me when I called. Chances are good it won't be here next Halloween, but then neither will I."

As we look at the wall, the familiar stone-like shimmer dropped into a pond, heralds the arrival of the door. It pops into place as if it had always been there.

He smiles when he sees the dragon's head doorknob. "You're definitely the key. What is it? I guess it's not magic."

"What's magic, anyway? Medicine looks like magic if you go back far enough."

"I wanted it to be magic. Everyone lives such brutal lives, trying to find magic or what we can call magic. What is it then?"

"We really don't know," I say. "It's a human construct, not natural. We know that much. Government? Maybe, but which one? Military? Probably or will be. How it got here is a mystery even to the scary-smart people I know. Maybe it's an escape hatch. God knows what this planet is going to look like in the next fifty years. Hell, the next five years! But I'll keep digging. Nothing stays secret forever. Not even that we were visited by extra-terrestrials."

"Really?"

"No, I was joking. Physicists are mean jokers."

He stands, leaning on the cane. He hugs me; I hug him back. It feels real and good. "How do I go in alone? Have you figured it out?"

"I'm coming too."

"Oh, now, wait a minute," he says. "You can't leave everything behind."

"Don't give me that shit. You're not my boss or my father. I wouldn't let them tell me what to do either. And there's a chance I'll get my hair back once we go through."

"I'm not going to look for you this time. I'll shun every stranger. I can't come back to this."

"No matter what happens, I'll do the same. There comes a time when you have to rebel."

"Then how will you get back?"

"I'll think of something," I say. "There are bound to be other doors in other places. Maybe I'll end up in Switzerland. Get a job at CERN. Whoever runs this world owes me that much."

On the way to the door, I help him along.

"You do the honors," he says.

I grab the doorknob. He places his hand on mine, just like every other time. I feel the familiar pulse of energy coursing into me, making my shoulder ache. I twist the knob and pull the door open, taking a step back as it swings toward us. Bright sunshine this time, as if early morning. I squint and see the path twisting off around the bend. A warm wind touched with the fragrance of exotic flowers, and I take a deep breath. He stands taller, straighter.

"After you," I say.

This time. The door shuts behind us with a solid *thunk*.

Washington Daily Echo: Wednesday, 17 March

WHISTLEBLOWER ALLEGES DEATH SQUAD ACTIVITY

(AP) – The Senate Intelligence Committee began hearings into decades-long clandestine research conducted by a consortium of international paramilitary organizations. A whistleblower complaint from a private think tank in Meyrin, Switzerland ignited a furor in congress when it was learned U.S. citizens were targeted by death squads financed by...

THE LAST DOOR IN THE HILBERT HOTEL

Evvan Land

Two blurry splotches leaned over me—one green, one blue. Above them, a dark figure hovered.

"Get up, it's starting soon. What's your name?" Green said. Or maybe it was Blue.

It's Alo— My head pounded. *Alogon. You can call me Allo, though.* The splotches coalesced into a cyan smear. *What's starting?* I blinked my surroundings into focus.

Green separated from the cyan smear. The two strangers standing over me wore black academic robes and colored masks. Green's mask grimaced, the cheekbones jutted out, and the corners of the eyes were pulled into sharp crow's-feet. Blue's mask was nearly featureless, with only eye holes and thin, baby blue lips. They gave me a sense of comfort that offset the pounding in my head and slight dizziness.

"Come on," Green said and pulled me to my feet.

We stood in a grand hall, reminiscent of a Roman basilica.

Doors tiled the walls as if each doorframe had been glued to its neighbors. A crystalline table split the rococo hall in two, scattering prismatic patterns throughout, and I was unable to find either end of the hall or the head of the shimmering table. It was magnificent.

On the long wall across the table, a giant lectern rose from a stage. On the long wall behind me, an enormous clock stood sentry. Hundreds of clock hands wound at various speeds, some counterclockwise, so figuring out the time was impossible. Its ticking boomed relentlessly in my ears. Glaring at the thing only worsened my headache.

We stood alone at the table, while robed figures, all wearing masks, stood by some of the doors. Confused by it all, I turned to Blue for an explanation and fired off a list of questions. *Why was I laying here? How long had I been out? How did I get here?*

Blue ignored me, distracted by the figure floating overhead.

My head still pounded, and I rubbed my temples. I felt the edge of a mask.

"Masks stay on!" More dark figures gathered, hovering over us.

"Right." Blue held up his hands in deference. "We just got here—we didn't know."

Can someone tell me what's going on?

"InCreds," Blue said. "Best to avoid them. I'm Logen. And this is Idris." He pointed at Green. "How're you feeling, Allo?"

Not great. I had the shakes and felt nauseated.

Behind us, a door slammed shut, and the sound echoed through the hall. When I turned, all the doors were closed. Back on the other side of the table, a single door opened, but no one appeared.

All at once, all the doors on both sides of the table opened. More robed figures trickled into the great hall and stood side-by-side in front of their doors. Slam, slam, slam! For a moment, the ticking and slamming synched, which didn't help the gears in my head one bit.

"Maybe someone should close that one," Logen said, pointing at an errant open door.

"Move away from the table and get back in line," snapped one of the floating figures.

Logen and Idris supported me, and we shuffled toward the clock wall. Words, or word fragments, had been carved into the wooden floor. Codswallop. Help. Light. Lob. Apsis... The words were legion. Words that for some reason inspired dread and promise. Yet they were utter nonsense.

When we neared the clock, I let go of the others. *I'm feeling much better. Thanks.*

"Allo, no need for bravado." Logen gave me a pat on the back. "There's a saying, 'It isn't about what knocks you down; it's about *how* you get back up.' Anyway, this is us."

He pointed at the lintels over the three doors beside the clock. The lintel in front of me read 42, but the others were blank. I looked at Logen, confused.

"Give it a second," he said. A moment later, his lintel produced 41.999, which began scrolling a series of 9's.

"Same here," Idris said. "Only mine's 42 point zero forever." He drew a line through the air and pointed at the lintel between theirs. "This one must be yours."

Mine didn't scroll.

42? Anyway, aren't these all the same number?

The clock chimed beside Idris, and my head pounded in time.

"Welcomed," a voice boomed.

Welcomed?

Logen tugged on my sleeve, pulled me in line.

"Welcomed to Hell." A titanic, bearded man wearing a white robe took the far stage and grasped the lectern.

Hell? I turned to Logen. *Is this a joke? I can't be in Hell.* Logen put his hand on my shoulder. *Don't.* I pushed him away.

"I will be Janus Ordo." The titanic man's voice shook my soul. "This is the Starting Place. The Litmus Test will begin shortly ago." He chuckled to himself.

This is a dream, right?

Idris shrugged. "Hush."

No, it was madness. I was a good person, wasn't I? Wasn't I? I couldn't recall! In fact, I couldn't recall anything.

A giant woman wearing a white robe joined Janus on the stage, cradling a baby. A naked man of normal height, though barely to the giants' knees, confidently moved across the stage and stood against the wall to Janus's left. He shielded himself with a blood-soaked sword.

"My wife Epilo and our daughter, Hope." Janus took the infant. "Your proprietor in this afterlife will be Fugen Boniface." Janus balked at the naked man. "Due to Fugen's diligence, we conduct these tests uninterrupted within the Hilbert Hotel."

The words "Hilbert Hotel" rang like a desk bell that fails to summon its bellhop. I should've known that name. I should've really known that.

Janus thundered on. "His InCreds protect the Lobachevsky roundtable and the credibility of The Litmus Test." He pointed at the crystalline table, which didn't look at all round.

Fugen aimed the bloody sword at the floating hooded figures, the InCreds. They drew clubs from their robes, thrust them over their heads, and grunted in unison.

"They've suspended their belief indefinitely," Janus said. "Due to their unique state of credulity, the safety of the Lobachevsky roundtable and our ability to conduct the tests will be thanks to them."

It was time to wake up. Hell didn't have hotels or tests or floating psychopaths saluting a naked man. Then again, that sounded hellish.

"Our motto here is, 'Let your light shine.'" Epilo tapped her fingertips together with the ticking of the clock. "A word of caution—if you approach the Lobachevsky roundtable," she said with stolid indifference, "the InCreds will snuff out the light of your soul."

Hope cried.

I was trapped. InCreds cast ominous shadows over everyone.

"Hush, deary," Epilo said. "The Litmus Test is your only opportunity to prove yourself worthy or whether you're destined for worse." She pointed to the clock. "You must find The Exit before time is up. If you are able, you may leave. It's easy to get lost in the Monty Halls, and whoever loses their mask cannot exit. Fugen?"

"Okay." Fugen cleared his throat. "Abandon all hope, ye who enter here. It's nice to see so many faces. I feel like I already know each and every one of you." Even at a distance, Fugen's stare unnerved me. "It's okay if you don't find The Exit. It's a veritable impossibility. It's nice here. We have all-you-can-eat buffets, interesting people, and every day will be unique. If only slightly."

Epilo stomped, shaking the room. Fugen went silent.

"Look," Logen pointed to the far side of the Lobachevsky roundtable. "Somebody came through that door."

Indeed, someone had. He joined the line, glancing back at his door several times. Something flashed in his hands.

Janus scowled at Fugen and retook the lectern. "Through your doors, you will find the first of the many Monty Halls. You may have begun!"

The clock rang, and my head pounded. Throughout the hall, doors slammed as others left and began their tests. All but the one that had just entered. He sprinted across the room towards the table. Towards me. Several InCreds drew their clubs and intercepted the runner. I couldn't bear the thought of the InCreds extinguishing someone's light. But I was powerless to stop them.

What do we do?

A door on my left slammed. Idris had already left the Starting Place.

"Are you coming?" Logen opened his door, and he left too.

Wait!

I abandoned the poor soul to his fate and hurried through door 42. The hallway was full of closed doors with no end in sight—the Monty Hall. It was empty aside from Logen and Idris. Each lintel read, "Try Me."

"This little light of mine... I'm a little light of mind." Several doors away, Idris was singing.

The ticking of the clock rang through the hallway.

Do you hear that?

"Of course," Idris said.

"This iteration has begun," Logen said, shutting my door behind me.

"I'm running out of time," Idris sang.

Where is everyone else?

I opened door 42 again, but instead of the Starting Place, it opened into a poorly lit room. Inside, a chess set demanded an opening move.

What the...? Where's the Starting Place? I'd almost closed the door when a glint of light caught my attention. As I peered inside, a sinistral eye slid into view through the crack of the door and leered back. I slammed the door closed.

The lintel still read, "Try me." I tried the door again. This time, a robed figure was opening a door that led into another Monty Hall, and beyond that, another figure, another door, another hallway—seemingly infinite. I slammed it shut. Frenzied, I opened and closed the door several times, and each time it opened, it revealed a different room.

"Allo, relax," Logen said.

Relax? How are we supposed to find The Exit if you can't trust the doors!

"We don't have time for this again..." Logen said. "We need to try *something* no one else has tried. I think we really need to try—"

"Okay," Idris said. "We'll try *something*." He opened door 42 again and barged through the doorway.

"I meant the roof!" Logen clasped my hand and dragged me along.

Sensual red light pulsed throughout the room. People danced to the din of an all-bass tune punctuated by gasps and moans. Couples and triples writhed together. I feared I'd stick to something—or someone—I was unfortunate enough to touch. Glancing around, all the masks bore expressions of anguish and sorrow, and Idris's mask was nowhere to be seen.

I'm not sure we should be here.

"Just help me find Idris," Logen said. "It's better if we stay together. There's no way to know where any given door leads. We need a better vantage point." He led me to a vanity covered in shards of broken mirror.

I swept aside the broken glass and climbed up. On the other side of the room, I spotted Idris stuck to several half-naked dancers wearing nothing but plaid skirts.

"Did you find him?" Logen asked.

I pointed in Idris's direction and climbed off the desk.

"Okay, stay here while I get him," Logen said. "Don't. Go. Anywhere."

Just hurry.

After Logen left, the dance crowd swelled. A dozen hands tugged at me, at my robes, at my arms and legs. One even tried pulling off my mask. I backed away and bumped into the vanity.

Mirror shards fell to the floor, and I carefully returned the bigger pieces to the vanity but kept hold of a dagger-shaped fragment. It had power in a room filled with supple threats.

Reflected in the shard, a dragon-masked figure slinked up behind me. I hid the fragment inside my robe pocket and spun to meet them.

"Are you testing?" A young woman swayed to the music, wearing only a dragon mask and a plaid skirt. She let out a faint moan. "Why don't you stay awhile?" she said, sliding her hands up and down her glistening torso.

I swallowed hard and tried not to gawk.

It's certainly tempting.

She danced closer. Her cognac and lavender scent intoxicated me, and for a moment, the drumming of the clock subsided.

Maybe I will stay awhile.

She ran both hands up and down my arms, and my body swayed with hers.

"Come on." She pulled me toward the spit-exchange corner. I could've stayed in the moment forever. Her hands slid up the back of my neck, and she reached for my mask, pressing against me, pressing the shard into my ribs. Sharp pain sobered me.

I grabbed her hands. *Masks stay on. It's against the rules.*

I pushed her away and found Idris and Logen waiting by the open door.

"Did you get lost?" Idris said.

I looked back at the girl I'd left standing in the corner. *I'm not sure.*

Idris, Logen, and I re-entered the Monty Hall, closed the door, and slumped back. The girl's cognac and lavender scent lingered, but I felt more alone than ever.

And lost. All around me, endless possibilities. Or were the doors endless improbabilities? Either way, I didn't know our next move.

"You can't disappear again, Idris," Logen said.

"Well, you said we had to try *something*. So, I'm trying." Idris opened the next door. He quickly slammed the door and moved to the next.

"Sure, like no one's tried *that* before." Logen threw up his hands. "Maybe someone will just show us the roof."

You guys need to stop arguing. We don't know how much time we have, and we just wasted a bunch in there.

"*Was* it a waste of time?" Logen said. "Ever forward."

"I'm not arguing," Idris said. "I choose this one." He swung open another door and disappeared through it.

Bloody hell.

Logen and I dashed after him. Again.

Instead of a den of passion, a fiery orange room opened before us. Centered in the room, two sawhorses supported a wooden door, creating a makeshift table. Various delicacies presented a feast. A far cry from the luminous Lobachevsky table. I licked my lips.

Passed out at the far end of the table, someone wearing a pig mask hunched over, collapsed in a chair. Indifferent, Idris gorged himself as he made his way toward Pigface.

Jeez, Idris. Need a napkin?

"Perhaps you need a napkin too." Logen wiped the drool from my chin. "Idris, please stop."

"Welcome! Please, help yourself!" Pigface said, sitting up. "I haven't had a guest in quite some time. Well, Parsimony."

Logen and I paused, but Idris continued eating.

We're looking for the roof. Where can we find the stairs?

"Oh, please eat. I insist." Pigface gestured at the cuisine.

An awkward moment of silence passed.

"Ah, I've got it—you're testing," Pigface said. "You should meet Parsimony." He stood, revealing a dragon mask draped over his chair. His robe flared open, betraying a surprisingly frail body. "Cursed with a big mouth and a small stomach." I reeled at his slovenliness, but I pitied him in his perfectly tailored misery. "Follow me," he said.

Idris shoved a few more donuts into his robe pocket, and we followed Pigface out of the room and down the Monty Hall.

"In here," Pigface said, holding open a new door. "Hey, Pars!"

Idris rushed in before us.

Why does he have to do that every time?

"He doesn't know any better," Logen said. "But if he didn't charge forward, who would?"

We entered an emerald green room reeking of clove and cinnamon incense. In the corner, a pile of assorted masks rose like a throne. A button-nosed, rosy-cheeked blonde woman perched on top. She wore a white top with a plaid skirt, like a sorority uniform, and toyed with a harlequin mask. Her lithe body held a commanding presence, yet alone and vulnerable, in need of someone.

Idris stood motionless under her gaze. As did I.

"Isn't there a film where a princess wears other people's faces for disguise?" Idris whispered.

"Not princess, assassin," Logen whispered back.

Guys, shut up. Don't be rude.

"This is Parsimony," Pigface said. "And this is—" Pigface turned to us and paused. "Another iteration of the test. We were... dining."

Jelly donut filling dripped from Idris's cheek on to the floor.

"You gave him some food?" She squinted at Pigface. "What if *I* wanted some, and it was the same some that'd been eaten?"

"I-It's fine," Pigface stuttered. "They're guests."

Parsimony's face tensed for a moment, and she waved her hand dismissively at Pigface. He backed away, bowing.

"So, you're taking the Litmus Test," Parsimony said.

Yes. And we're trying to get to the roof. I pointed at the ceiling. *Do you know the way?*

"What's wrong with him?" Parsimony asked Pigface, cocking her head to the side.

Nothing.

Pigface shrugged.

"R-ight. Up. There's no up." Parsimony shook her head. "There's no right or left or down either." To Pigface, she raised her eyebrows and said, "What are you expecting me to do?"

"Pars, come on," Pigface said. "I think he means The Exit. You can spare a little more compassion than that."

"I've never found it," Parsimony said. "I don't even think there is An Exit. But maybe we can help each other. You know, make a... trade?" She twirled the mask in her hands.

"Would Barren know?" Pigface said.

The harlequin mask fell from Parsimony's hand and fractured on the floor. "That was my favorite one." She took a deep breath. "Yes, Barren might know. Good idea, *Pigface*. You'll surely be rewarded."

Parsimony stepped down from the throne of masks and pressed the wrinkles from her skirt. As she came closer, I caught a faint lavender scent. My pulse quickened. My breath came shallow. More threatening than the InCreds. My instinct was to retreat, but I remained rooted, lingering on the contours of her face one awkward moment too long.

I cleared my throat. *You don't wear a mask?*

"Is there something on my face?" Parsimony touched her cheek and blushed. "Oh, I took off my mask a long time ago. I've stopped caring if there's an exit. That whole 'this is our daughter, Hope' spiel is bogus, anyway. Janus and Epilo act out the same thing over and over."

She had given up. I brushed a lock of hair out of Parsimony's face.

We're going to find The Exit. You should come with us. We'll find a way for you to escape too. I wasn't sure how, but I'd find a way.

"Helping each other it is then," Parsimony said. "Let's go meet Barren."

"Barren!" Idris shouted and lurched to the door.

I stepped in his path. *We're following her lead now.*

Idris gave me a cockeyed stare.

Parsimony led us past a row of hanging masks—a dog, concentric diamonds, a smiling pink face, a dragon—and into the Monty Hall.

"Barren?" Parsimony said, flinging open a door.

Idris shoved past me and disappeared through the door.

I turned to Logen. *That's not going to happen again.*

"Good," Logen said. "We're making progress."

Inside the room, the walls were lined with chalkboards full of equations—mostly illegible—signed *BH* or ending in *codswallop*. A large Indian rug depicting the Mandelbrot set covered the bulk of the floor. In the corner, wearing a mask of black and white concentric circles, another robed figure scribbled feverishly at his desk.

"What are you doing, Barren?" Parsimony said.

"Yeah, what are you doing?" Pigface parroted.

"Oh, great." Barren let out a huff. "Let yourselves right in, Pars. I *was* writing the proof of my intelligence. Now, I'm talking to you."

Parsimony walked around the room, scanning the chalkboards. She stopped at a conclusion Barren had circled.

"What?" She held her head in her hands. "Is that...?"

"Yes. I finished," Barren said, puffing his chest.

What is it?

"Did the others believe?" Parsimony shook her head in disbelief.

"Well, no. They still think I'm a dipshit," Barren said. "They say, 'Only a dipshit would suggest attempting to get past the InCreds.' This is why I'm writing this proof of my intelligence." He gestured at the scrawls on his desk.

But what is it?

"I thought," Barren said, "if I could write a proof, establishing that I'm not dipshit, the others would believe. So, I started the proof: If I'm to believe the others, then I'm a dipshit, which I don't want to believe, so I'll assume that it's false. Premise α_1 is then assumed to be false. Here, I apply the law of Parsimony—no relation. Thus, I find that the more beliefs of the others that I declare unlikely—and all of their α_n opinions are that I'm a dipshit—the less likely it is that it's *unlikely* I'm a dipshit. So, therefore it's more likely I'm a dipshit. But if I believe that I'm a dipshit by following my own logic, then I shouldn't believe my logic because I'm a dipshit. And therefore, I'm not a dipshit."

"He's a dipshit," Idris said.

"I know, I know," Barren said. "I've been here too long, and nothing makes sense anymore. I hate the others. They make me doubt myself. They made me question whether the entirety of mathematics crumbles in on itself tautologically. Nonsensically. Codswallop."

Poor Barren. His mind was wound forwards and backward at the same time. Like a clock with too many hands, telling the correct time and the wrong time, all at the same time. Yet another private perdition, closing in like the circles on his mask, eventually culminating in his surrender.

I didn't want to end up like that, trapped and comfortable in my own hell.

He looked at me for a moment and nodded. "I was in your position—trying to find The Exit. No cigar, but I was able to write a proof that The Exit exists. Here." Barren reached into a desk drawer and pulled an orange 8x12 envelope, revealing a dragon mask underneath.

I touched my mask, wondering what it looked like. I turned to Parsimony. *How do people get their masks?* She shrugged, her eyes dull with sorrow.

"This is it." Barren held out the envelope, averting his eyes. The envelope read, *On the Non-Non-Existence of The Exit by Barren Habenicht.* "Take it. Maybe it'll do you some good. I know it by heart."

I accepted the envelope and tried to comfort him, but he recoiled.

Parsimony, this is what we need. There really is an Exit. Come with us.

"It's time for you to go now." Barren gestured at the rug.

Idris went for the door. I blocked him.

"Move." Idris pushed his mask against mine.

His weight threatened to overpower me, and he could probably take me, but I was done letting his impulses dictate our path. I locked eyes with him. He had a cold resolve. Mine burned.

"Okay. Jeez." Idris stepped back. After a moment, I stepped back too. We had a new understanding.

Besides, that's not what Barren meant. Here. I threw the rug aside, revealing a hatch door.

"Hey, look at that," Parsimony said. "A hidden door." Her face went from consternation to wide-eyed anticipation.

No more barreling through doors. From now on, Parsimony points the way.

Idris looked to Logen, who nodded and said, "It's time."

"Has this always been here?" Pigface said, peering at the hatch.

"Recent development," Barren said. "If I know one thing, you won't find The Exit in the Monty Hall."

How do you know? We were sent to the Monty Hall.

"It's all in the proof," Barren said, pointing to the envelope.

Logen rubbed his temples. Idris nodded.

*Maybe this is the **something** nobody has tried before.*

"It's worth a shot," Logen said.

"We'll see about that." Parsimony crossed her arms.

We had everything we needed. I hoped. I opened the hatch door, and inside, a ladder descended through darkness to a dimly lit landing. I signaled to Pigface to head down, then Logen, then Idris. Before Parsimony and I slipped through the hatch, I pointed at the equations on the chalkboard.

*What is **this**?*

Parsimony pointed at *codswallop*. Of course. She moved to the hatch, revealing three scribbles: time remaining < time needed; apsis = Lobachevsky; failure = eternity?

Is this why Barren despairs? Why you gave up?

Parsimony smiled at me. "It's our turn."

Why don't I go first in case there's danger?

She climbed down first, ignoring my offer. Her confidence bolstered mine.

"Good luck," Barren said. He closed the hatch and we descended into darkness, Barren's ominous calculus still burning in my mind.

The ladder went on forever into a room filled whispers. A faint luminescence hovering near the floor gave us bearing until something momentarily obstructed the light.

"We're not alone down here," Logen said. "Everyone be careful."

When we reached the bottom, the light blinked out. The darkness was complete. I stood motionless, one hand still clenching the ladder.

Childish giggling and pitter-patter echoed in the void.

Definitely. Not. Alone.

The light reappeared, momentarily blinding me. Nothing more than a warm radiance, it bobbed in the air and giggled.

"Boo."

I ducked reflexively. Aside from the light, there was no form, no shape. It had all the contrivance of an elaborate hoax, and yet, I could feel its radiance.

W-what are you?

"I'm Ailia. Janus and Epilo's mother, or daughter," she said in a voice like rain and wind chimes.

A dark figure, featureless like a homunculus and the size of a 4-year-old boy, ran and hid behind Ailia's light.

Ailia chuckled. "This is Nolla. He's my twin."

What little form Nolla did have melted into an inky puddle, then recollected into a spot, black, as though someone had punched a hole into the fabric of spacetime.

"You shouldn't fraternize with humans, sister," he said, in a voice like a dissonant piano chord.

"We've been shut in here for eternity," Ailia said, "because we told Janus and Epilo that they're our children. And they just couldn't believe we couldn't believe that they didn't believe us."

But what are you? Angels? You're obviously not like me.

"I'm Nolla's inverse," Ailia said.

"Is Nolla you're inverse?" Logen asked.

Ailia tittered. "Nolla's nothing."

"I see," Logen said.

"No, you don't," Idris said.

Ailia brightened. "For *something* to have an inverse, it must first *be*. *Nothing* must take form first before it can have an inverse. Nolla took form. For me to be his inverse, I must have no form."

None of us quite understood. Why wasn't anything ever simple? I held the proof up in one hand. *Why would Barren send us down here?*

"Yeah," said Pigface, "why don't we read the proof?"

"Why bother?" Parsimony said. "We wouldn't understand the math."

"Math proof?" Ailia brightened. "If it's math, Nolla and I can help."

"That's fortunate," Parsimony said, still struggling to believe. I spread the proof on the floor for everyone to read.

"No, sister," Nolla said. "No more humans after last time."

"You need to let it go, Nolla," Ailia replied and hovered over the pages.

What happened last time?

"I wandered the Monty Halls with humans," Ailia said. "It was so much fun."

"That's not the point," Nolla said. "Nothing good happens when humans claim they *know* something about something."

"What do you have against humans?" asked Pigface.

"Humans are binary," Nolla said. "Even your words are just ones and zeroes—Mom, Dad. Yes, no. To be or not to be."

So what? Aren't you binary?

"Yes, so what?" Nolla said. "Human logic is flawed. When presented with the choice between right and wrong, humans will *choose* to do wrong, even when they know what's right." The tenor in Nolla's voice darkened. "I have no faith in humans."

"You're so incredulous sometimes," Ailia said. "I've read the proof. Are you ready?"

Yes, I'm ready.

"Get on with it," Parsimony said.

"Barren defines every state of the universe," Ailia said. "These states take on a probability distribution. Essentially, he's proven that the chance of the universe taking on any 'state' is effectively zero. And the summation of infinitely many such states is still, somehow, one."

*It's like the Hilbert Hotel. The chance of picking the **right** door to the **right** place is basically zero.*

"That's what I was thinking." Logen nodded.

"Good job, human," Ailia said.

"Ailia!" Nolla screeched.

"He's already figured it out," Ailia said.

Parsimony looked at me, eyes wide with excitement.

"No. He has not," Nolla said.

"Well, one 'state' claims otherwise," Ailia said.

"Probability zero. Remember?" Nolla said.

"I think this is a map," Logen said. "According to this very confusing proof, *every* 'event' could be considered an exit depending on the 'state.'"

So, any door can be The Exit?

"The probability *is* zero," Parsimony said, rolling her eyes. "I've checked every door."

"This proves it. There is indeed an exit," Ailia said. After a moment of silence, she added, "I'm going with them."

A faint ticking entered the void, and my head began to throb. *We need to get going.*

"No, Ailia. You *won't!*" Nolla expanded. "We already have everything between us. You won't leave me alone. There is no Exit. This is no proof!" An arc of plasma shot from him to the pages, igniting them.

Flaming pages of Barren's proof disappeared inside Nolla's growing sphere. More purple plasma arced from the blackbody, incinerating the remaining pages and striking nearby.

The darkness pulled at us, and we struggled against it.

"Grab the ladder!" Logen said, grasping it himself. Idris was already climbing.

Pigface squealed. He struggled to keep his footing. Parsimony extended her hand but could reach only his mask. His feet lifted from the ground, and Pigface flew into the darkness, leaving a horrific silence.

Parsimony's eyes filled with desperation. She clutched Pigface's mask. The void pulled.

I hooked my foot on the bottom rung and stretched. *Take my hand.*

She tried but slipped, mask in hand. I hooked my fingers through the mask's eyehole and pulled. She held fast, her determined fingers clutching the other eyehole. She scrambled over me onto the ladder.

Nolla's event horizon continued to expand, pushing darkness outward, pulling our light inward, threatening to devour us all.

Climb!

Idris and Ailia were already near the top. She shined down the ladder to light our way. Parsimony scurried up.

"Let's go," Logen said.

GO! I'm right behind you.

Nolla's darkness consumed the lower rungs of the ladder, his eternal emptiness crushing ever closer. My heart raced. My arms ached. I was the last one left. Only a few more rungs, but I had no strength to climb. Time was running out.

"A little closer!" Parsimony held out her hand.

Everything went dark. I flailed for purchase, finding nothing. Even if I'd had strength, I couldn't find her hand. I was lost to the darkness. At least I got Parsimony out.

"This little light of mine..." Idris sang.

Ailia grew blindingly bright, my personal supernova. The shadow cast by Parsimony's hand became my beacon.

Even here, in the depths of Hell, there was a shred of hope. I marshaled my last iota of strength—my light still shines!—and seized Parsimony's hand. I pulled myself up and scrambled out. The hatch door slammed shut, and Idris dropped to the door.

"... I'm gunna let it shine." He smiled.

We found ourselves in a black antechamber. Ailia's glow settled.

I scooted toward Parsimony. *You saved me!*

"You saved me," Parsimony said. "That's a first." It didn't seem to bring her any comfort. She still held the pig mask.

I'm sorry I couldn't save him too. I turned to Ailia. *What happened to him?*

"He's gone where infinity comes to rest." Ailia spoke with a sorrowful measure.

"No one's ever gotten this far before," Parsimony said. She stood by me and rested her head against my shoulder. "This place scares me."

The room held nothing notable. Until I looked up.

A glass dome capped the antechamber, and beyond the glass ceiling lay the expanse of space. The only visible stars belonged to an aged lenticular galaxy. A yellow tendril from a nearby sulfuric nebula coiled around its center as if it would snuff out the galaxy's light any second.

Logen stared at the ceiling and said, "Do you remember a universe filled with galaxies? All the other galaxies have drifted away with the expansion of space. Memories lost to us."

Parsimony squeezed my arm, still shaking. We, the forgotten damned, mourned a soul I'd barely befriended, someone who struggled like everyone else. It seemed I knew him.

Despite all that'd just happened, there was a perfection in this moment of solace, right here beside Parsimony, another stranger that I was timelessly and wistfully bound. For the first time, I felt calm. If the moment could've lasted for eternity, I would've accepted.

We're lucky. Most people never get a moment like this.

"Possibility zero." Parsimony let go of my arm and turned her back to me.

My eyes stung with tears, and I looked away. It really was Hell. *Don't worry. We'll find the Exit, and I'll find a way to get you out.*

"Is this the roof?" Idris said.

"Looks like there is no roof." Logen scanned the room. "But where's The Exit?"

"There's no Exit here." Ailia hovered near a corner, revealing a corridor previously hidden in shadow.

We followed Parsimony and Ailia through the corridor that opened into a sparsely furnished room. On the far side of the room was a door, and in the corner, light glinted off polished steel. A sword leaned against a small table with a chess set.

On a huge sofa, a woman and man sprawled beneath a bedsheet. The woman had deep features, and a blotted bandage covered her right eye. Beside her lay Fugen Boniface.

"Fugen?" Parsimony said.

The woman shrieked, pulling the sheet up to her neck, and Fugen fell to the floor, naked. She stood, securing her bandage, and wrapped the sheet around herself like a toga.

"What are *they* doing here, Fugen? *She* can't be here. Get her out. Now!"

"Nice to see you too, Justine," Parsimony said.

"How did you get in here?" Fugen stood, towering over us.

"Wouldn't you like to know?" Parsimony said.

Does it matter how we got here? It only matters that we're here. I pointed at the door. *That's **The Exit**, right?*

"That's the exit from this room, not *The Exit*." Fugen laughed.

"Fugen, get them out of here," Justine said. "Having the Inverse here will bring the wrath of Janus and Epilo! And you!" She spat at

Parsimony. "You still haven't paid for stealing my sword. Where's the justice in that?"

Parsimony glared back.

"Calm yourself, Justine!" Fugen stepped between them. "Besides, it's too late. They're already here." He turned to me. "Let's start over. Everyone, this is Alogon, a repeat tester."

"I'm reporting this to Janus." Justine stomped to the door and threw it open. Beyond the door, InCreds hovered over a robed figure on the far side of the Lobachevsky table.

"Close it. Now." Fugen gritted his teeth. "If everything stays in here, only we know the truth."

Justine slammed the door shut and huffed. She crossed her arms and fell back into the corner in protest.

Did you guys see that?

Logen and Idris mumbled to one another. "We can't help you anymore," Logen told me.

Fugen smiled, sucking air between his teeth. He gestured at the empty sofa, inviting Parsimony and me to sit. With some reluctance, we accepted his offer while Justine continued to fume.

"So, you're taking the Life Test," Fugen said.

Litmus Test.

"He's taking the Litmus Test," Parsimony snapped.

"Care for a game?" Fugen nodded to us.

Just then, the door opened. A beam of bright light cut into the room. As we waited for the intruder to reveal themselves, Justine glanced at her sword across the room. The door closed all but a sliver. She peeked through the crack with her good eye, her sinistral eye, and the door slammed shut. She snapped around, a look of terror on her face. Her one eye fixed on me.

The staccato of the clock returned, making my head throb.

"You should play Justine sometime." Fugen carried the chess table to the sofa. "I've yet to beat her."

The chessboard was ready. I was white.

There was a familiarity here. Each piece had potential move sets, every piece a tester, every move a choice, every space a set of doors. Chess was a journey for knights and queens, kings and pawns. At some point, I may have been good at this.

"You see," Fugen rotated the board around, "the Life Test is very much like chess." It was now Fugen's move. "You have to do something. Make a move. Pick a door. Call check or be silent." He opened with white pawn to E4. "Let's make a deal. If you win, I'll tell you where The Exit is. If I win, you give up your quest for The Exit and immediately join the ranks of the InCreds."

I turned to Parsimony, searching for a source of courage. She smiled, weakly.

"I'll be right by your side," she said.

Deal. I responded with black pawn to C5.

"My move then." Fugen scanned the board. "Let's examine the knight. He moves awkwardly but is loyal to the King. You may have encountered some of these people in The LT." White kingside knight to F3. Black pawn to D6. "Then there are those who charge in without a plan." White Pawn to D4. Black pawn takes D4. "Be wary of these soft-headed peons. Every move you make should further your goal to win the game. To find The Exit." Knight takes black pawn on D4.

Fugen's white knight now controlled the center of the board. I pondered my options, then played knight to F6. Now he'd have to react to me.

"Sometimes you can anticipate a problem, so the best thing to do is take prophylactic measures." He mirrored my move with knight to C3. Expecting him to advance his knight, I moved pawn to G6.

I'd made a mistake. Fugen knew the game better than me. My palms grew clammy.

"Very good," he said condescendingly. "Sometimes there are things that you *must* do, even if there are better things we could be doing. But always remember your goal." He moved his queenside bishop to E3, and I saw now that I was losing the fight for position. I'd need a miracle to win this game. Black kingside bishop to G7. "Protect what's important to you while moving towards your goal." Pawn to F3. He closed off the kingside. I guarded my own goal with a kingside castle. "Someday, you may even find a powerful queen who will protect your interests." He moved his queen forward one space to reinforce the frontline knight and bishop.

I was trapped. There were no good moves.

Parsimony reached out and moved queenside knight up. I looked at her, confused.

"You see," Fugen said, "Parsimony is playing her own game. A bigger game." He moved his bishop to C4, completing the phalanx formation.

Parsimony rolled her eyes and moved our—*her?*—bishop to D7 defending the knight.

"She wants to play both sides. Do you think she's helping you? She's here to take the game. Then no one can find The Exit." He castled on the queenside.

"What is it you think I want?" Parsimony moved rook to B8.

"You want everything." Fugen pushed his pawn to H4. "Allo, if you win, she gets exactly what she's always wanted. She gets to know where The Exit is. If she controls it, nobody will ever leave again. She doesn't want to leave. And she'd never let you leave, either." He reached under the sofa, pulled out a dragon mask, and set it on Parsimony's lap. "Recognize this, Allo? This one is hers. Mmm... smells like lavender."

I looked at Parsimony, dumbfounded. *You were the temptress?*

"Don't stare at me like that."

Tell me it wasn't you. It's not true, right?

"She's more than a temptress," Fugen said. "She is all things greed and heiress to the lower echelon. What do you think she traded her mask for? You want truth, Allo? What truth are you looking for? That your life had meaning? That you're a latter-day mathematician trapped in a coma? Or that you're anything more than a rounding error in the cosmic calculus?"

What do you mean? I couldn't breathe. I was more than a miscalculation. More than a traded piece on a cosmic chessboard. But I found myself frozen, lost, alone. Debris drifting in space.

I reached to Parsimony for a lifeline to tether me. She appeared on the verge of professing her innocence, but those words didn't come.

"I wish you would speak, Allo. Anything," she said.

"I'm afraid he cannot." Fugen's lips curled into a sinister grin. "Only the upper echelon can hear his thoughts, and you don't rank high enough."

My thoughts? I drifted yet farther away. *Logen?*

Logen looked at his feet.

"The truth is," Fugen said, "you can't always get what you want, Parsimony. You and I both know he would never accept you as you are."

Parsimony turned to me. "Is the idea of being together so awful?"

I wanted the answer to be 'no.' I wanted to take back a few

moves. Back to the antechamber. Back to that perfect moment that receded away like those distant galaxies. But the pieces had already been traded. *You lied this whole time.*

Tears welled in her eyes. She steeled her trembling lip and reached for another piece. I stopped her. I grabbed my queen and moved it to A5.

"Ah, well played," Fugen said. "Now I have tough choices to make. Do I advance the trusty knight in retaliation and sacrifice the queen, or do I move the queen, sacrificing the knight? Which piece will I move? Which door will I choose?"

Fugen must've reached for the wrong piece.

"Enough!" Justine leaped over Fugen, swinging the sword, smashing the chess-set and table. She raised the sword above her head. "You can't win the game. No one gets to The Exit."

I pulled the glass shard from my robes.

"You brought a knife to sword fight?" Fugen said.

Ailia!

Ailia directed a blinding beam at the shard that then reflected into Justine's vengeful eye.

Ducking the sword, I crawled towards the door. Fugen tripped over me, taking Lady Justice down with him.

"You're too late." Fugen burst into laughter. "There isn't enough time."

I kicked away from them. Idris and Logen, my allies, my friends, waved and dematerialized into green and blue splotches. I turned to Parsimony and croaked out, "Good. Bye."

She threw the dragon mask, and it crashed against the wall beside me.

I scrambled to my feet and ran through the doorway into a Monty Hall. A baby's cries echoed, and every lintel read, "Wrong Way."

Still holding the mirror shard, I finally dared to look. My mask was transparent. I laughed. Had it been cyan before? Or had it always been transparent, right in front of me, like the carvings on the floor, like Barren's chalkboard...? Apsis = Lobachevsky. Hope giggled.

"I know where The Exit is," I said, cracking open the nearest door. Inside the Starting Place, the Lobachevsky table glistened— The Exit.

"The Litmus Test will begin shortly ago." Janus chuckled at his own joke. The giggling ceased. In a few moments, Epilo would go on stage.

After a few deep breaths, I recomposed myself.

Epilo said, "A word of caution... if you approach the Lobachevsky roundtable..." Tick. Tick. "... InCreds will snuff out the light of your soul." Hope cried.

Was there any time left? Time. Time. Time! I had failed. Probability zero.

No. Individually, each attempt is insignificant, but the summation of all states is somehow—one.

I entered the grand hall and stepped in line with the others standing at attention. The room shook.

Janus called out, "Through your doors, you will find the first of the many Monty Halls. You may have begun!"

When the other testers left through their doors, I ran. I ran as fast as I could. The InCreds turned, drawing their clubs in unison. I dropped to my knees. Every iteration must add something new—a failure, codswallop—so it goes unnoticed. Eventually, the failures lead to success.

Using the shard, I carved "Lobachevsky apsis" by a "codswallop." On the opposite side of the table—The Exit—testers were leaving. *I* was leaving. Maybe I could get a message to myself.

"WAIT!!" I called. The door on the far side closed. One of the InCreds swooped down, knocking me to the floor. "Go to Hell!"

I lost consciousness. Perhaps for a moment, perhaps longer.

My head pounded. Three splotches leaned over me. One green, one blue, and another darker figure. "Get up," Green said. "It's starting soon."

THE WENDING WAY

J. S. ARTZ

Aristreal had felt the call coming for an age, like an ache in her bones that crept in slowly over time. She pulled her cloak tight around her shoulders and ventured out to check the boundaries of their land for news that was bound to be bad. First wars, then fires, plague, drought, and oppression—the list of transgressions humans wrought against the goddess Maka's sacred lands went on and on. Now the earth shook at regular intervals as if to confirm all of Aris's fears. When everything they'd done to try to Shift the mortals on Earth had failed, all the warnings falling on deaf ears, the Seers would leave. It was known. They'd be called, and they would go. As it had been foretold.

Aris walked the fields skirting the cedar forest, thinking, thinking. Of what came next and what shape it might take. Would she even recognize the home she'd left aeons before? Her memories of the far distant realm were shrouded in shadow, dimmed as Aris's own eyesight had dimmed over ages spent under the harsh light of the sun blazing through a depleted atmosphere. But a tiny spark of memory remained, a vague feeling of safety and warmth. The susurrations of peaceful, unpolluted seas lapping at crystalline shores. Maka standing tall before her, holding her hand, and whispering as Aris strained to dip her toes into the sea. But what had the Mother said? Aris couldn't quite recall.

When she reached the twisted big-leaf maple at the westernmost corner of the land she and Kai had called home these many years, Aris looked up into the bare branches and whooped softly under her breath. A pair of piercing amber eyes caught hers. In a silent explosion of wings, Pöllö burst from her roost and soared down to the patch of canvas stitched onto the shoulder of Aris's cloak.

Aris chucked the owl's beak with the knuckle of her forefinger and searched her pouches for a small hunk of dried meat. She'd rescued the Spotted Owl as an owlet, no more than a fist-sized ball of gray fluff, from a tangle of monofilament left at the edge of Kachess Lake. The bird's second toe still bore the scar, though she'd grown strong enough to fledge three broods over the past several breeding seasons. Aris had since seen a reduction in rodents scavenging her grain stores.

"What news, my friend?" she asked, running a finger over Pöllö's sleek brown plumage.

The owl moved her head from side to side, as if trying to decipher the Seer's words. Aris closed her eyes, focusing on her intention, and the owl quieted. Images flashed in Aris' mind of birds fleeing inland, some heading north despite the waning of the season. Of bright flares of color on the horizon, an image that might be beautiful if not for the forests crackling with flames and suffocating smoke. It was as she'd feared. The end was coming. Her joints throbbed with it, both the knowing and the dread.

"Thank you," she said. She paused before adding, "I must go soon. I'll miss you, little one."

The owl clicked her beak at Aris and leaped from her shoulder. One wingtip brushed Aris's cheek as the owl swooped low across the forest's edge, eyes trained on the ground.

"Happy hunting," Aris whispered.

Her walk took her next to the bald-topped boulder that stood watch over the north end of their property. The glacial erratic had held court on their land since roughly the last ice age. Now, the stone was glowing, an unearthly light radiating from its solid granite center. Aris had not needed another sign to Know, to See, and yet here it was.

They had been younger when the glaciers receded and deposited the rock on this particular piece of land. The creases in their skin more like a system of trickling creeks than the canyons that furrowed their brows in these dark days. Back then the dangers had come from both deep within the earth and beyond the protection of the atmosphere, rather than from the bipedal beasts themselves. But over time, the humans had organized well enough to spread and thrive and consume and conquer. Their ambition eventually morphed from survival into a greed-filled, grasping aberration that no amount of power could Shift. Though goddess knows the Seers had tried.

In that long-ago time, the placement of the rock had grounded them, told them this would be where they'd stay until the next phase, whatever that would be. And they had. Stayed. And watched. For a time, life had been all bliss and wonder, she and Kai, hand in hand. But then their youthful hope slowly turned into something darker.

Aris ran a gnarled hand over a patch of moss a little too bright green to be natural on the surface of the immense boulder. The earth trembled as if in response. Yes. It might be nice to rest her bones. To sit with Kai on those sparkling shores and not have to summon the strength to fight against the inevitable flow of the human tide. The moss glowed brighter under her touch, so she picked away at it, exposing runes beneath. Runes that hadn't been there before. Runes sent from Maka to Aris and Kai and the handful of other Seers who, having failed to stem that tide, had stayed to Witness its final cycle.

It was hard to watch something fail in slow motion over a millennium. And Aris was tired. But not too tired to decipher the message.

All Seers bound for Maka's shores
Seek a door through time and space.
When Blue Moon casts her brightest light
Glowing runes will guide the way.

She could almost hear the Mother's cryptic voice chanting the words. Calling to her. An age had passed since she had felt either hope or peace. But soon they would find both.

"What are you doing out there?" a voice called from the door to their dwelling, just beyond the boulder's shadow. Kaidar. Ever-faithful. "A storm is brewing."

As if he'd conjured the storm himself, thunder rumbled and lightning flashed on the distant horizon.

"Yes, indeed," Aris said, more to herself than to Kai. "You don't know the half of it." She turned from the runes and headed toward their dwelling. The Blue Moon would rise on the third morning hence. There was much to consider before then.

Kai waited for her at the door. "You're usually the first to head for cover when the clouds darken."

"I was distracted by the clicking of limbs at the forest's edge."

"A portent?"

"I'm not sure yet," Aris said, turning away to re-braid her silver hair in the small mirror by the door. She never kept things from Kai, but when she parted her lips to speak, her throat thickened. The words did not want to come. Not yet.

His hand on her shoulder stopped her braiding and closed her mouth. And she couldn't avoid his searching eyes in the reflection. "Come, share some wine with me. You don't have to scry for the answer right this second."

"I'm not scrying," Aris said, heat rising in her cold cheeks. "The wind tussled my hair."

"It doesn't take the wind to do that," he said with a smile, still watching her in the mirror.

Her lips tugged upwards, responding to the familiar pattern of banter between them. Her hair was wild, full of spring and spiral. Wild like her spirit. A spirit ready to journey. But what of her companion?

Kai would go with her. But would he regret it? He was the one who held out hope for this planet even as he watched hers fade like the autumn leaves, becoming brittle, and floating away on the wind. Spring would bring no renewal for that hope; it had been held too long and lost too slowly to be revived by a simple change of season.

And she had lost too much. Her hope and it's source.

She would not think of the boy. She could not. Not now. But she did need to see him. Despite the storm.

"I'm going to gather a bit of oregano and thyme for the soup," she said.

"You haven't even tasted it yet," Kai said, frowning.

"I can smell what it needs," she said, walking back out the door.

Kai had been right about the storm. She'd been so focused on the boulder that she hadn't seen the clouds darken, hadn't noticed the changing light. A storm was always brewing in this place as autumn fell, the restless energy propelling the land toward winter, always simmering on the edge of a raging downpour.

She stepped through the low rock wall on a worn path that led to a small stone set in the ground. No name. No date. Instead, Kai had smoothed a place in the rock where she had then placed the ring. He'd given her the ring to commemorate their only son's birth a hundred years ago. A simple silver band with a deep blue stone, a symbol of the dearest thing their bond had created.

Lukus.

And he was the greatest of the things this world had taken from her. Her beloved son. Which was why she'd be pleased to step through the door. To leave this world to choke on its own poisoned ashes.

The runes had promised the end would be coming soon.

Her eyes had Seen enough. They were ready for a rest.

"You're not here," she said, placing her hand on the rock's surface. "But you are with me always, my child." She clenched her fist and pulled it to her heart.

As if in answer, the wind lifted her braid from her shoulder, letting it settle over her hand. And the rock glowed. Of course, she'd hewn it from the same erratic, and it too contained the magic of Maka's message.

Your journey's end arrives at last
As hope allays and fire brims.
You've Witnessed all, now See the End
Time runs short for Shifting Fate.

"Yes, yes, of course," she said to the rock. "Three days. If it were three beats of a hummingbird's heart, I would go this second."

But was Kai as anxious as she was to go? And could he leave their son? Their home? Their hope? She closed her eyes, searching for an answer on the wind. But the chaos of whispers offered no easy solution.

The storm unleashed its pounding wrath, and she returned to Kai with empty hands. He didn't bother asking about the herbs. That's how it was with a partnership of aeons—Kai knew where Aris had been. He didn't yet know what had stirred her secret pain and driven her there, but Aris would tell him when she was ready. It had always been their way.

When would she be ready, though? There was not much time.

The soup tasted bland for lack of seasoning, but neither of them spoke of it. And when he poured her an inky black cup of blackberry wine, she accepted it despite the beginnings of a headache.

As the thunder stampeded toward them, wind and rain lashed the trees outside their home. Aris stared into her cup. She let her eyes lose their focus and took a deep breath, tasting the earthy remnants of the soup and the sweet tang of wine on the air. And when she peered into the cup, the world around her dissolved.

She hadn't meant to scry, but there she was in the shadow world. It was risky dipping below the surface of reality during a storm, especially when an even bigger one was headed their way. But still, she needed to know if her Mother would be pleased with what her youngest daughter had accomplished these aeons past.

A flicker of memory took her back to her childhood home's sparkling shores. To a youngling eager for adventure and impatient with her mother's final lecture, impatient to be on her way. All the talk of Witnessing and Shifting had seemed so tedious at the time.

Now Aris searched the dregs of memory for some clue. Surely, she had earned the right to walk through that door. Doubt flickered in her mind—Earth had changed her. No impartial observer sat here now in weathered boots. She had chosen a different path, one that bound her to this place, when she'd made a child here. A piece of her immortality lay beneath the cold ground, withering to dust and bare bone. So, instead of shedding the world's darkness, she had let it seep into her skin like the autumn rain seeps into the cracked dirt when the dry season comes to an end.

Aris focused her attention on the Seers who dwelt in other parts of the world. Morrigan would stay to watch it all burn, to stoke the flames herself. It was her way. But what of Cerridwen? Shapes moved in the misty gloaming, stepping one by one out of the world she had known and onto the Wending Way. Each Seer fizzed and faded like a light snuffed out, making the shadowed space even darker until a burst of flame wiped it clean.

Images flashed quickly before her eyes. Scenes of death, chaos, destruction. It would be a relief to avoid bearing Witness to those final moments. And yet a second potentiality emerged. A far-off light remained alone in the murky black. One that was familiar to her. Mielikki. She might stay. And Tapio with her. Tucked into the northernmost corner of the safest part of the world. They would never give up their forests. Their people.

Then Lukus's fever-bright eyes flashed before her mind's eye, mouth turned down, accusing, as he'd been in the final hours of his affliction. She was not giving up their people, the trees he loved, the land he'd once roamed like the wild thing he had been. She was giving up the world that had taken him from her. *But that same world had given rise to his creation in the first place.* She could almost hear him say the words.

"I will not argue with ghosts," she shouted into the darkness. But that didn't stop the Knowing. That Lukus would want her to stay to the bitter end. To fight rather than rest. It had always been his way. So like his mother, Kai always said.

The mists of the in-between cleared, a scene resolving into sharp focus. She was on the beach again, staring at the night sky with Maka by her side. And this time, the words were clear.

"Some stars slowly fade, my child. And others burn bright until their end, exploding into the stuff of more, perhaps even greater stars."

"What kind of star am I?" she'd asked, grinning at her own cleverness.

"Oh, my love," Maka had said, taking Aris's small hand. "No one could accuse you of fading away quietly. You will burn bright as the greatest supernova, even to the end."

Aris had laughed in delight at the thought. But no smile tugged at her lips now.

"Come back to me, Aris." Kai's fingers brushed her arm.

She startled, sloshing the purplish wine over the thick rim of her cup. She paused a breath to let her eyes refocus until she saw the concern in his crinkled brow.

"I'm here now," she said.

And yet, when he led her to the bed they'd shared for an age and took her solace there, the words still wouldn't come, though they pulsed in time with the beat of her heart. *It's time. It's time.*

The next morning, Aris woke to a cold bed. She'd slept late, past dawn in an autumn where first light was hours later than it had been just weeks previous. A glance out the window revealed Kai, standing at the boulder, leaves and branches from the storm scattered at his feet. His hand outstretched toward the glowing runes. She hadn't told him, and now he had discovered the cause of the lump in her throat, the scrying, the silence. As he always did, without her saying a word. She dressed quickly, fingers fumbling with her laces as a fevered pulse thrummed in her veins.

The grass lay flat and wet from the storm, the petrichor alive in the air. Aris joined Kai at the erratic. The runes were still there. And some new ones glowed beneath yesterday's verses.

Make haste again through this stone door
If you choose to find your peace.
The chance to travel onward wanes
When the moonlight fades at dawn.

"Kai, I—" Her thoughts were too complicated to distill. She took a breath of cool autumn air.

"Would you have snuck out in the moonlight and disappeared like an imp in the night?" The lightness of his words belied their deeper meaning.

Without him, he meant. Would she have left without him?

"No," she whispered. Then louder, surer, "No. I thought you might not want to go. Might not want to leave him behind."

Kai's black hair whipped in the wind, as his eyes sought hers. "You are the only home I have ever known. And I promised Maka on the day we left that I would see you through when the end came."

"Why have I never heard this?" She stared at him. She was not the only secret-keeper then. They could still surprise each other even after an age.

"It seemed like parental foolishness at the time," Kai said, staring into the distance. "And then it faded into memory."

"Tell me." She pulled him down onto the ground, making a

seat of her cloak to keep the wet grass from seeping through to their limbs.

"The Seers were all preparing to go." He draped an arm over her shoulder to pull her closer. "And you were so anxious to get here, to see the new earth and watch the tiny cells coalesce again and again into creatures as wonderful and complex as what generations past had Seen on their own Sight Journeys elsewhere."

"Mother wanted me to stay by her side, immortal and safe." Aris dropped her head to his shoulder, letting her eyes fall closed, so she could wade through shadow to dredge up the long-forgotten memory. "But still she let me go."

"You've never been one for safety," Kai said. "But I think she blamed me: As if you'd chosen me over her."

"Oh no, she surely blamed only me," Aris said with a harsh dry laugh. "She knew best of all how impossible it was to dissuade me once I'd set my mind to something."

"Yes, she told me that I couldn't stop you from your purpose," Kai said. "As if I'd ever try to hold you back."

Aris paused then, considering his words. And Maka's. Because though her Mother loved riddles, this smacked of prophecy. "Can you recall exactly what she said?"

"It was an age ago," Kai said. "And my memories have faded."

"Try," Aris said. "For me."

He plucked a seed head from the grass and twirled it between his fingers before he spoke. "You can ask her yourself in a few days," he said. "Your Mother never forgets."

And never speaks without purpose. "Humor me," Aris said.

"It was just after our bonding ceremony. She'd visited each of the Seer pairs to bestow a blessing. And you, of course, had run off, escaping the formality of the occasion for the freedom of the forest."

"The sea, actually," Aris said, smiling at the memory of diving into waves so ice-cold they stole her breath. "Go on."

"She said that no one else could help you survive what was to come. That no one else would see your purpose in the end and help you reach it."

"Mother knew from the beginning how steady you were, how you balanced me." Aris reached for his hand, mulling over his words, and Maka's.

He let her twine her fingers in his. "She must have foreseen the plague and all we would suffer. And still, she let you go."

"Always concerned with my higher purpose," she said, more to herself than to Kai. "But what of the lives we're leaving behind?"

Kai frowned then. "Nothing will keep me from returning Home now that we've been called. What is there to leave behind besides bitter memories?"

Aris expected relief at the words. It didn't come. He would go. They would go together. Of course, they would. Their hearts both bore as many scars as Earth herself. But there were more than just bitter memories here. And was he misreading her Mother's words an aeon ago?

She searched his eyes and found no doubt there. But her doubts flickered brighter.

"Let us prepare our goodbye," Kai said. It was what the runes dictated. So why did the words make her so uneasy? How did he not see the truth in the Mother's words? That her purpose and his were no longer one. "Come, I'll gather the herbs this time."

"Yes," she said, smiling at the forgotten oregano despite her heavy thoughts. "Meet me at the pool. I'll gather what is needed from my herbiary."

Aris selected the items she'd need from her neatly organized

workspace in the corner of their cooking room. Rows of bottles
and jars full of herbs, tinctures, and salves had been gathered and
brewed and preserved each season, varying only by what had grown
particularly well that year. She'd have to leave them all behind, of
course, but then again, she wouldn't need medicine in the undying
lands.

She pulled down a basket and filled it with a candle, a bundle
of rosemary and lavender, a vial of moonlit water, a hunk of quartz,
a bit of blue yarn, and her athame. She stopped by Lukus's rock,
lifting the ring from its place and tucking it, too, into her basket
as a plan took shape in her mind's eye.

Kai stood by the pond. So still he was, she thought for a moment
that he'd tried her scrying. But his magic was of a different sort.
She Saw so that he could Shift. Such subtle messages he'd crafted
to those mortals. And age by age, they denied him. Ignored him.

He looked up as she approached, only deep in thought after
all. She unpacked her basket as he studied the murky surface of
the pool. The storm had obscured the water's usual reflection but
would hopefully not obscure her Sight. As the ceremonial smoke
drifted over the surface of the pond, she placed her crystal, the
vial of moonlit water, the candle, and a branch from her beloved
cedar at the points of the compass. Then she and Kai stood over
the bundle of herbs and whispered their goodbyes to the earth
they had known together.

Kai took the horn-handled athame from the sheath at her side
and waved it to the four points, thanking the earth, wind, air, and
fire for all that it had given them in their time on Earth. Aris's
chest tightened as Kai moved the knife, severing his connection
to this place. And then he whispered something not meant for
her ears—the quiet apology and the name. Lukus. Tears welled

in her eyes. He would leave their son. And so would she. It had been foretold, after all.

She took the dagger from him and repeated the motions. But the spell called for focus on the bonds to be severed, and her thoughts scattered instead, torn between this world and the beyond. When she tied the blue yarn around the bundle and blew out the candle, a crackle of electricity raced up the backs of her legs.

"You'll place it on his grave, then?" Kai asked of their goodbye charm.

Aris looked down, half a nod. Only once Kai had turned his back did her intention focus into a point sharp as her dagger's. Despite her weary eyes, her scarred heart, she would burn bright enough one last time to Shift what he could not. And if she failed, she would lend the star-stuff of her immortality to the universe, birthing new worlds in the wake of this one that might fail. She slipped the ring from the basket and secured it to the bundle with the bit of blue wool.

After repacking her basket, she walked once more to the boulder erratic. New runes had appeared in the night.

You've given all your mortal years
Helping those who ruined all.
You've earned your rest with toil and loss.
Find your way to Maka's home.

I understand now, Mother. I do. These words are not for me.
"Take care of him," she whispered into the bundle of herbs. She made the final ceremonial cut in the air above the bundle and tucked it into her robes. It was done. Her decision made.

She did not return to Lukus's grave.

They kept watch for the moon on that final night. Together.

Neither able to sleep in the darkness. Neither ready to break the silence between them. What more could be said?

And so, they made their way to the boulder in the cold light of the pre-dawn moon. The runes disappeared, and in their place, a black nothingness emerged. It was not as Aris had imagined. Not the light-strewn path on which they had arrived ages past. Kai must have had the same doubt, for he reached for her hand. She took it, then pulled him to her, breathing in his smell of cedar and earth.

He would stay with her to the end, in this place they had loved, if she asked. But could she let him stay? Aris released her grip on Kai and faced the nothingness of the door before her, her gut tugging her backward, away.

She slipped the bundle of herbs from her pocket and fiddled with the yarn.

Kai's hand warmed her shoulder, and she looked up. Her throat thickened again with all the words she might have said. Her lower lip trembled as she sucked in a ragged breath, and his eyes widened. She held the bundle out to him with a shaking hand.

He clenched his fist as if refusing to take the charm would stop what was happening.

"I spent too long convincing you that hope was lost and forgot to convince myself," she said. "Kai, please take it with you."

Kai's eyes glistened in the silvery moonlight.

"Please," she whispered.

His fingers unfurled slowly. An act of will.

"I know better than to try to sway your mind." The words were raw, as if they cost him dearly, which only made the lump in her throat sink down enough to encase her aching heart.

"And better than to suggest you forego paradise for my sake," she said.

He nodded once. "I would have followed you to the end," he said. He would have stayed, and she could not let him. His pupils widened then. He Saw her purpose. And his own.

They tumbled into each other, arms that had held each other for an age, grasping in desperation, holding on, squeezing tight. Their hearts beat together for one more breath before a wisp of cloud across the moon reminded them that time was ever short. Their journey together had reached its end.

He released her, and she bit her lip to stop herself from crying out. With one last tender look her way, he turned toward the boulder's gaping maw. Before she could whisper, *I'm sorry*, he stepped forward and was swept into the void, clutching the goodbye charm as he vanished.

The tears welling in her eyes spilled down her cheeks. Then the moon retreated behind a cloud, and the door to paradise turned once more to solid rock, the interruption in the mossy coat the only hint of where runes had glowed just minutes before.

A screech pierced the dawn, and Pöllö landed on her shoulder in a flurry of wings. "You knew it was not a long goodbye, then, friend," Aris said, and Pöllö clicked her beak as if in response.

They turned together toward the horizon, which shone with the eerie orange of the coming fire. The ground trembled under her feet, enough that the owl dug her talons into the canvas. But Aris rolled her shoulders back and prepared to Travel. Her journey would not take her home—that way was closed to her now—but it would take her onwards, to the other side of this earth. She would stop the fall if she could with the others she would find there. And if they could not Shift, they would Witness. Together. It was as it had been foretold. She had been called. And she would go. It was known.

ABOUT THE AUTHORS

Susanna Skarland is an editor, author, and unicorn, holding an M.F.A. in writing for children and young adults from Hamline University. She is a member of SCBWI and volunteers for PNWA and the Society of Young Inklings, providing editorial support. Susanna writes fantastical, adventurous fiction about ancient dragons and flighty faeries. A sucker for playful language, she flagrantly fashions fanciful fractal fricatives. All of Susanna's stories weave in a strong thread of science and the natural world, the residual effect of a substantial career in biological research. Her home is under the clouds of the Pacific Northwest, where you will find her with a cup of tea in hand and a cat underfoot.

Elle Blackwood is a writer, poet, and editor with a bachelor's degree in creative writing and English literature. She is the author of *A Map of My Existence*, an autobiographical poetry collection first published in 2018 under her pseudonym Elle Wonders. When crafting prose, Elle writes magical realism and literary Gothic fiction infused with folklore. She creates landscapes of dark woodlands, lochs, and rugged moors, with old mansions and thatched cottages that serve as central characters. Elle lives in a small Victorian river town with her husband, son, and a big black poodle with a penchant for solving mysteries. When she is not writing, Elle is painting, traipsing through old graveyards in search of lost stories, or browsing antique shops. She collects obscure antiquarian books, lonely teacups, and vintage photographs of people she doesn't know.

Erik Amundsen is from a small Norwegian village north of the Arctic Circle. Surrounded by forests, mountains, and fjords, he spent his youth hiking, fishing, and cross-country skiing. When he wasn't outdoors, he had a book in his hand, reading mysteries and westerns before he was old enough to start school. After college, Erik lived in Oslo, worked in IT, and became a genealogy researcher. He had nearly forgotten about books until he moved to the U.S. and married a writer. Erik lives with his family in the Pacific Northwest, where he's surrounded by forests, mountains, and fjords. He has over 70,000 relatives in his family tree.

J. S. Artz spent her young life sneaking into wardrobes searching for Narnia. When people started thinking that was creepy, she had to find other ways to explore her passion for mystical adventures. Now she finds those long-sought doors to magical story worlds in her work as an author, developmental editor, and book coach. An active member of the writing community, she volunteers for SCBWI and Pitch Wars and is a member of EFA and AWP. Julie lives in an enchanted forest outside of Redmond, Washington, with her husband, two strong-willed teenagers, and a couple of naughty furry familiars.

R. L. Castle writes science fiction, fantasy, and speculative fiction—from robotics and elementary particle physics to dragons and wizards. He has a soft spot for writing realistic family dynamics, despite fantastical settings and circumstances, and slays the page with love and loss. He holds an M.F.A. in writing for children and young adults from Hamline University and writes in all forms for young readers and adults alike. When not writing, he can be found battling monsters on Pokémon Go.

Steve Garriott has always been a voracious reader and writer. He enjoys all genres of fiction and non-fiction, with a special love for books about Presidents Lincoln and Grant, and the works of Mark Twain and Kurt Vonnegut. In 2016, Steve's three submissions were chosen as the winners of the Everett Public Library flash fiction contest. He has navigated ships, taught writing to high school students and adults, been a corporate trainer, and currently works as a technical writer. A regular participant in National Novel Writing Month, Steve has numerous unfinished novels scattered on flash drives.

Carlos Joaquin Gonzalez is a Chicano writer who grew up in a household filled with music and books. He became absorbed in storytelling at a very young age, and being half Mexican mestizo, half European-American, he has two distinct cultures to draw from. An autodidact by nature, Carlos has been a lifelong historian and is fascinated with alternate history. Aside from writing and researching, he loves grunge music, concerts, and single-malt Scotch. Carlos is majoring in Chicano Studies at the University of Washington and will graduate in 2021.

Evvan Land is a writer who grew up immersed in storytelling of all kinds—through books, role-playing games, movies, and a wicked sense of humor. Evvan is drawn to philosophical ponderings, mathematical proofs, and astrophysics. When he's not writing or calculating, you can find him playing piano, practicing Japanese, reading, and eating peanut butter. A Pacific Northwest resident at heart, Evvan is pursuing a degree in Mathematics from the University of Colorado, Boulder.

Karin Larsen fell in love with writing during a childhood filled with arts and music in the American Midwest. She pursued a degree in sacred music, combining writing and music composition to create and direct a stage musical for her capstone project. When fibromyalgia ruled out the world of collegiate-level teaching after a few years, she turned her energy towards her family and faith communities. She now works as music director of a small Lutheran church, and her writing often focuses on family and relationship dynamics. She lives in the state of Washington with spouse Keith and daughter Phoenix.

Bobbie Peyton is a writer of Filipino and European heritage. Born in the Philippines, she moved to the United States as a baby and grew up in an idyllic small town in Oregon. Bobbie now lives in northern California with Tillman and Wonton, her two little (but ferocious) dogs, where you can find her at work on many writing projects, especially for younger readers. A former high school special education teacher, Bobbie has master's degrees from Tufts University and Hamline University's M.F.A. program in writing for children and young adults.

H. K. Porter is new to writing, but not to stories. She's been an avid reader since she was three years old and is currently an active member of two book clubs and National Novel Writing Month. In addition, she is a beta reader and provides critiques for the books of indie author and publisher, Heather Marie Reaves. Ms. Porter lives in the Pacific Northwest, and aside from reading, she loves cooking with her partner, gardening, and exploring thrift stores for unusual objects as inspiration for short stories.

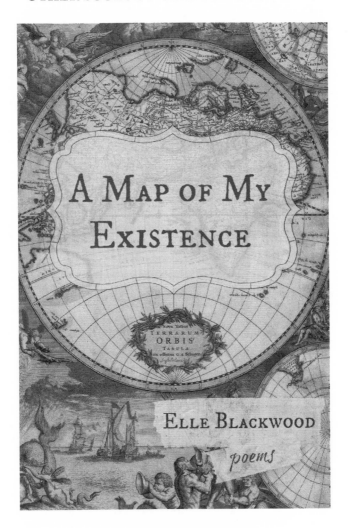

A MAP OF MY EXISTENCE

ELLE BLACKWOOD

poems

Some truths don't travel well.
Some of them die along the way and others
stray from the flock. These are a few who
survived the journey.

Made in the USA
Middletown, DE
18 December 2020